"The right man for you isn't on a dating site."

"How do you know?" Lydia retorted.

"I know because..." The tender expression in Gunner's eyes rocked her back on her heels. "You're a special lady in a category all by herself."

After all the teasing and mocking, Lydia wasn't sure she believed him.

"And," he continued, "if you open yourself up to new experiences, you might discover that what you thought you wanted in a man isn't what you want after all."

"What kinds of new experiences are you talking about?"

"Ever had a fling?"

She sucked in a quick breath. "No."

The air sizzled between them. Gunner Hardell wasn't her type—wasn't even close to the guys she'd been paired with on savvymatch.com—but there was no denying they were attracted to each other.

His gaze warmed and he tilted his head to the side so the brim of his cowboy hat didn't ████ ███ ██ the face.

"This isn't a goo███████████████████████zy that he hadn't he████████████████████

Dear Reader,

I've never tried an online dating site but I have friends and relatives who've joined them and found their perfect match. Those who didn't... Well, their dating stories would make great fodder for a book! As humans, we are always searching for perfection, for that one person who possesses characteristics and qualities we believe are a perfect match for us.

Needless to say, Gunner Hardell doesn't come close to the perfect match Lydia Canter is looking for in a husband. And Lydia's not the kind of woman laid-back cowboy Gunner is looking to have a long-term relationship with. Lydia and Gunner have their lives all mapped out until a night of fun leaves them grappling with an unplanned pregnancy.

I hope you enjoy watching Lydia and Gunner struggle to do what they believe is in the best interests of their child, only to discover that what they think they want isn't what they really need.

For more information on me and my books, I invite you to visit marinthomas.com. You can keep up-to-date on my current releases and promotional giveaways by signing up for my newsletter at bit.ly/marinthomasupdates.

Happy reading,

Marin

THE COWBOY'S ACCIDENTAL BABY

Marin Thomas

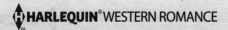

ISBN-13: 978-0-373-75760-2

The Cowboy's Accidental Baby

Printed in U.S.A.

Marin Thomas grew up in the Midwest, then attended college at the U of A in Tucson, Arizona, where she earned a BA in radio-TV and played basketball for the Lady Wildcats. Following graduation, she married her college sweetheart in the historic Little Chapel of the West in Las Vegas, Nevada. Recent empty-nesters Marin and her husband now live in Texas, where cattle is king, cowboys are plentiful and pickups rule the road. Visit her on the web at marinthomas.com.

Books by Marin Thomas

Harlequin American Romance

Cowboys of the Rio Grande

A Cowboy's Redemption
The Surgeon's Christmas Baby
A Cowboy's Claim

Rodeo Rebels

Rodeo Daddy
The Bull Rider's Secret
A Rodeo Man's Promise
Arizona Cowboy
A Cowboy's Duty
No Ordinary Cowboy

The Cash Brothers

The Cowboy Next Door
Twins Under the Christmas Tree
Her Secret Cowboy
The Cowboy's Destiny
True Blue Cowboy
A Cowboy of Her Own

Visit the Author Profile page
at Harlequin.com for more titles.

To all of my readers *waves* who can't get enough of my cowboy stories, which is a good thing since I really like writing them.

#Stampede #Texas #CowboysofStampedeTexas #LongLiveCowboys #Cowgirl #Cowboy #Boots #CountryMusic #Rodeo #BroncBusting #BullRiding #Romance #HappyEverAfter

Chapter One

"You ever seen a cowboy ride a bull, sweetheart?" Gunner Hardell winked at the sassy redhead he was flirting with Saturday afternoon in the Gold Buckle Bar—the best cowboy saloon in Mesquite, Texas.

"No." Eyes as big as the Lone Star State and brown as the muddy Rio Grande blinked at Gunner.

"Well, Pa…" Dang, what was her name? Patricia… Patsy… Pamela? "You're in for a real treat because—"

"Hardell, I got ten bucks that says you won't make it to eight."

The redhead forgotten, Gunner spun and grinned at the cowboy striding his way. "Watch and weep, Johnson." He crossed the squishy mat and made a big production of circling Diablo, the infamous bucking machine. The bar had purchased the mechanical bull a while ago, but Gunner had yet to test it out.

"Be careful!" Redhead whatever-her-name-was called out.

Johnson mimicked the buckle bunny and male chuckles erupted, but Gunner paid no mind. His competition was just jealous that the prettiest, sexiest girls gravitated toward him. While his buddies practiced their macho swaggering walks and sulky expressions,

Gunner smiled and treated the barflies like ladies, endearing himself to the opposite sex. The young women competed to be Gunner's one and only, but none had convinced him to trade in his bachelorhood for a pair of matching wedding bands.

Gunner eyed the bucking machine. After he'd entered the bar earlier, he'd hidden in the shadows and watched the big shots take turns on the ride. The bull was a far cry from a real one, but it snorted smoke and challenged the most athletic cowboys with three riding levels—easy, medium and insane. The GoPro camera that came with the machine displayed each ride on the high-definition video screens throughout the bar and Gunner couldn't wait to see how good he looked on TV.

"What'll it be, Hardell? Easy or insane?"

"You have to ask, Tex?"

The machine operator spoke into the microphone. "Gather round, folks, 'cause Gunner Hardell picked insane!"

The onlookers chanted, "Insane! Insane! Insane!"

Cowboys—the real ones and the wannabes—circled the mat and money exchanged hands.

Gunner swung his leg over the cowhide-covered machine. Bull riding wasn't his specialty. His almost-six-foot frame preferred broncs. He slid on a riding glove, then wrapped the rope around his hand before sliding forward and finding his center of gravity. He glanced at the redhead, whose hands were clasped together, and she seemed to be praying as if she were in church and not a cowboy honky-tonk.

Deep breath. Take another. Gunner closed his eyes and imagined the ride. As soon as he raised his hand and signaled that he was ready, Tex would flip the switch to Insane and the bull would do three things in rapid succession: rise up, pitch forward at a ninety-degree angle and swing left. The motion would then repeat in the opposite direction and launch its victim into the air.

If he had his way, Gunner would be the first that afternoon to go the distance.

He took one last deep breath and then raised his left hand. A moment later the machine jerked, and his stomach muscles tightened as he blocked out the noise of the crowd. The echo of his harsh breathing and the angry, high-pitched snorts from the machine were the only sounds reaching his ears.

He kept his seat during the first rotation and ticked off the seconds in his head. He reached five when Diablo pitched forward instead of spinning left like he'd anticipated. Gunner had no time to react as he suddenly flew forward and did a face-plant in the mat. Grinning, he got to his feet, picked up his hat and bowed to the ladies, who, bless their hearts, were cheering as if he'd won a gold buckle.

"You owe me ten bucks, Hardell," Johnson said.

"Yeah, yeah." When Gunner stepped off the mat, a waitress handed him a bottle of beer with a piece of paper shoved inside the neck.

"Compliments of Mac." Mac managed the bar. "The note's from your grandfather."

This couldn't be good. He fished out the folded paper. *Get your blasted backside home. We got trouble.*

Now what? Grandpa Emmett was always bellyaching about something. Gunner looked longingly at the beer before setting the bottle on the table. He turned to leave, but the redhead blocked his path. Her mouth puckered in a sexy pout. "You're not leaving, are you?"

"Sorry, sweet thing. Duty calls."

"Duty?"

He leaned in and whispered, "Grandpa Hardell is having one of his fits and he needs me."

Her eyes grew misty. "It's so sweet that you take care of your grandfather."

"Us Hardells are like that. Family comes first." In reality Gunner gave his eldest brother and grandfather a wide berth because both men were always in a bad mood. "Take care of yourself, sugar." He kissed the redhead's cheek because women went nuts when he did that. Ninety-nine percent of the time, a kiss on the cheek won him an invitation to accompany the lady home. Thanks to Gramps, he was flying solo today.

He stepped outside and squinted against the bright sunlight. It was the end of May and the temps were already inching toward ninety—another long, hot summer in South Texas.

Gunner climbed into his Chevy pickup and cranked the air-conditioning. The last time he'd checked in with his grandfather had been a week ago and the old man had been his usual grumpy self. Maybe Logan had done something to piss him off, which was a long shot, because Gunner's sainted older brother never did anything wrong.

He headed north on I-35. After fifteen miles the gas indicator light popped on. He took the next exit off the highway and pulled into a Valero gas station. A blue Honda Civic with Wisconsin plates sat parked at the pump in front of him. He felt bad for all the cheeseheads who had to suffer through the notoriously frigid dairyland winters.

He slid his credit card into the reader, then stuck the nozzle into the neck of the gas tank. While he waited, a pretty blonde stepped out of the convenience mart. A gust of wind blew her long hair in her face and she swatted the strands from her eyes. She was a few inches shorter than his six-foot frame, but her strides ate up the pavement—the lady was in a hurry to get to somewhere.

As she strolled past his pickup—without glancing his way—a sense of déjà vu hit him, but he couldn't recall where he might have met her. The gray slacks and silky blouse buttoned to her collarbone insisted she was all work and no play. Not his usual type.

She got into her car and drove off. As he watched the Civic head south, he contemplated following her—just to see if he could coax a smile from her. With his luck, Miss Badger State would have mace in her car and spray his face with it.

His phone beeped with a text message from Logan.

Grandpa's birthday's tomorrow. Buy him something from us.

K. Why does he want me to come home?

IDK He's been pissy since Amelia Rinehart stopped by.

The old woman was poking her nose into his grandfather's business again.

Be home soon.

Gunner stuffed the phone into his pants pocket and returned the gas nozzle to the holder, then went into the store and examined the souvenirs on display by the drink machine.

The options for birthday gifts were limited to bags of pecans, a faux-leather wallet with an image of the Texas state flag stamped on it, an Alamo snow globe, a wooden rattlesnake and an armadillo key chain. The rattler won—it fit his grandfather's personality.

"Eight dollars and sixty-six cents," the clerk said after Gunner set the snake and his fountain drink on the counter.

"Throw a pack of Marlboro on there." Gramps had quit smoking years ago but lit up on special occasions. Maybe the lung darts would settle the old man down.

Back in the pickup, he flipped on the radio and Johnny Cash's voice came through the speakers. The town of Stampede was only ten minutes up the highway. Three songs later he moved over to the shoulder, then turned onto the dirt road that led to Paradise Ranch, a.k.a. Ornery Acres. Gunner and his siblings had nicknamed the homestead after their grandfather's sunny disposition.

Grandpa Emmett had always been cantankerous, but he'd grown crabbier after Grandma Sara had passed away from cancer and then five years later Gunner's father had been struck by a car and killed while changing a flat tire on the side of the road. From that day on, Gramps had become almost impossible to live with.

Since Gunner and his brothers didn't have a mother—they had one, but she'd taken off before Grandma Sara had died—their father and then grandfather had been saddled with riding herd over three rowdy boys and Gramps had never been good at herding.

After he parked in front of the sprawling one-story wood-and-stone ranch house, he entered through the back door and stepped into the kitchen. Shuffling sounds came from the hallway and he quickly stuffed the bag with the cigarettes and wooden snake in it beneath the kitchen sink. Seconds later his grandfather walked into the room.

"The last time you looked that angry, I broke the handle on the upstairs toilet," Gunner said.

Gramps hitched his pants. "That woman's determined to shove me off the wagon."

Grandpa Emmett was an alcoholic—Gunner's father had been one, too. So far he and his brothers hadn't followed in the family tradition and Gunner planned on keeping it that way. Hoping to cajole his grandfather out of his bad mood, he said, "You want to eat out tomorrow for your birthday?"

"I'm too damned old to celebrate birthdays."

"Eighty-five is hardly old," Gunner teased. "You're practically a spring chicken."

"My private parts ain't sprung in years, boy."

"They've got little blue pills for that, Gramps. I can call Doc Jones and have him write you a prescription." His suggestion earned him another glare.

"What has Amelia Rinehart done this time to get your dander up?" The old woman had been best friends with Gunner's grandmother, but she rubbed Gramps the wrong way and no one knew why.

"That wackadoodle gets an idea in her head and she can't let it go."

"What idea?"

"She says the town needs a makeover."

"What kind of makeover?"

"She wants to spruce up the Moonlight Motel—" the old man's pointer finger wagged in front of Gunner's face "—because you've let it fall into disrepair."

"It doesn't make sense to give it a face-lift." Tourists had quit visiting Stampede years ago, instead bypassing the town and spending their money in nearby Mesquite and Rocky Point.

"If you ran the motel better, Amelia wouldn't be sticking her nose into our affairs."

Gunner admitted that his management skills could use a little work, but flirting with buckle bunnies, singing karaoke and riding Diablo were a heck of a lot more fun than babysitting a dumpy motel while waiting for a wayward traveler to rent a room. "Amelia can think it needs fixing up all she wants, but you own the property, so you can tell her to bug off and pester someone else."

"No, I can't."

Gunner started at the serious tone in the old man's voice. "Why not?"

"I never paid back the money I borrowed from Amelia to buy the motel for your grandmother."

"I thought the bank loaned you the money."

"The bank wouldn't give me a second loan."

"Second loan? What was the first?"

Gramps waved his hand in the air. "Never mind that. I owe Amelia $130,000 for the motel and I don't have the money to pay her. She says she'll forgive the loan if I let her fix it up."

"Who's footing the bill for the improvements?"

"She is."

"A waste of cash if you ask me," Gunner said.

"There's nothing I can do to stop her." His grandfather narrowed his eyes. "And you're going to help her."

"Help Amelia how?"

"Not Amelia. You're helping her niece renovate the motel. The sooner you get it fixed up, the sooner that old woman quits pestering me."

"What about my rodeo schedule?"

"You can chase the girls after you finish with the motel."

Gunner raised his hands in the air. "Why does everyone think I rodeo for the buckle bunnies and not for the broncs?"

"Maybe because you don't make any money at it."

He ignored his grandfather's quip and asked, "Which niece am I helping?" Amelia Rinehart had three nieces close to Gunner and his brothers' ages.

"Lydia Canter."

His memory recalled the unfriendly blonde at the gas station with Wisconsin plates on her car. No wonder he'd felt a sense of déjà vu at the Valero. He'd seen Lydia in church at her uncle's funeral years ago. She couldn't have been more than fifteen, but her hair had been the same pale blond and just as long.

Suddenly Gunner was thinking that the Moonlight Motel might need a face-lift after all.

"I CAN'T BELIEVE it's been nine years since I last visited Stampede." Lydia sat on the front porch of her great-aunt's brick Victorian. The home looked out of place in a town comprised mostly of single-story brick homes.

"A funeral is hardly considered a visit, dear."

Lydia's smile dimmed as she studied her grandmother's eldest sister. "Are you lonely, Aunt Amelia?"

"Sometimes, but Robert and I had fifty-two years together. More than many couples get these days."

"Mom sends her love," Lydia said.

"How is your mother?"

"Busy with work." Lydia's mother was always busy. Her career came first before family. Every once in a while Lydia suspected her mother was disappointed that her only child hadn't followed in her footsteps and become a lawyer, instead choosing a career in interior design.

Aunt Amelia was the eldest of the four Westin daughters and the only one living. Her three sisters had passed away in their seventies, each leaving behind an only child—a daughter. Lydia and her cousins, Scarlett and Sadie, had been named after their grandmothers. Aunt Amelia had never had children and Lydia thought it was sad that her great-aunt didn't have a granddaughter named after her.

Lydia reached inside her purse for a tissue and her aunt asked, "Are you feeling any better?"

"A little." When her aunt had phoned to summon Lydia to Texas, Lydia had just gotten home from a doctor's appointment, where she'd been diagnosed with an ear and sinus infection. The last thing she'd wanted to do was board a plane all stuffed up, but she hadn't had the heart to turn down her aunt's request—not after the generous check Amelia had sent Lydia for her college graduation. The money had paid off more than half her student-loan debt. Rather than risk her head exploding on the airplane, Lydia had driven from Wisconsin to Texas.

"The doctor put me on an antibiotic." She'd been prescribed two weeks' worth of heavy-duty meds, and although Lydia was feeling much better, she'd been told to take all of the pills until they were gone.

"Did you ever get rid of those antique school desks?" Lydia remembered playing with her cousins in the attic when their families visited Stampede together in the summers.

"I have them. I wish Sadie would bring her boys to visit. They'd love playing on the third floor."

"Being a single parent is tough. Sadie spends most of her free time shuffling Tommy and Tyler to and from their activities."

"How often do you get together with your cousins?"

"We try to have a girls' night out once a month. And Scarlett and I trade off attending the twins' extra-curricular activities."

"I'm glad you three are close. I have fond memories of growing up with my sisters." Amelia smiled. "We caused our fair share of trouble."

"Grandma said you were the ringleader."

Amelia laughed. "Sometimes, but not always. Your grandmother hogged the bathroom every morning and made us late for school most days."

"I'm glad you kept this house after Uncle Robert passed away."

"I'll never forget the first time I met him," Amelia said. "I was sweaty, dusty, and my hair windblown after chasing our hound dog all the way into town. Barney was an escape artist and Father threatened to get rid of him if we couldn't keep him in the yard." Amelia poked Lydia's shoulder. "Your grandmother was supposed to watch him that day, but she'd snuck off with a girlfriend. Thank goodness I happened to step outside right when Barney chewed through his leash and ran off."

Lydia had heard this story before from her grandmother but kept quiet so her great-aunt could spin her tale. "I looked like a rag doll by the time I found Robert sharing an ice-cream cone with Barney in front of the Woolworth building. I was about to call out for the dog when Robert glanced up and our gazes connected."

"What did you think when you first saw Uncle Robert?"

"I'd never seen a more handsome, well-dressed man in my entire life."

Lydia's mother had told her that Uncle Robert had been an up-and-coming executive for Shell Oil when he'd passed through Stampede and had swept eighteen-year-old Amelia off her feet.

"I thanked him for entertaining Barney and went on my way. It wasn't until later that I heard about an oilman checking out the area and learned that man was the one who'd caught Barney." Amelia stared into space as if reliving the past, then blinked and smiled at Lydia. "I'm sorry things didn't work out with your boyfriend, Ryan."

It had been over a year since the relationship had ended and Lydia was ready to move on. "I joined an online dating service." She'd paid for the subscription a week before her aunt requested her help. Lydia had only had time to create her profile before packing her suitcase and driving south.

"The internet isn't safe. A young girl as pretty as you should be able to find a man without the help of a computer."

Lydia's fingers curled into her palms. "It's difficult to socialize and meet people when you're on a tight budget and trying to get a business off the ground."

"I don't understand why you left the company you were working for. What was the name of that place? Design..."

"Design Logistics. I quit because I wanted control over my work." What she'd really wanted was credit for her designs. Lydia's boss, Ellen, hadn't allowed her to meet with clients. It was by accident that she'd discovered Ellen had been taking credit for Lydia's ideas. When she requested a raise and was turned down, she'd struck out on her own and learned the hard way that it wasn't easy winning new clients when you had no references.

"What about meeting eligible bachelors through Sadie's and Scarlett's friends?" her aunt asked.

"It's not easy finding someone you're compatible with."

"All this talk about compatibility is ridiculous. Your uncle and I were raised very differently, but we made it work."

"I work out of my apartment, which makes it even more challenging to meet new people." And to add salt to the wound, Lydia's friends from college were all married and starting families. She was the odd woman out, resulting in awkward get-togethers when talk turned to babies, mortgages and the cost of day care.

"What kind of man interests you?"

"Aunt Amelia, I'd rather not talk about my dismal dating life." She flashed a halfhearted smile. "Can we discuss why I'm here?" What she really needed to be doing was focusing her time and energy on building her client base.

Amelia pointed to the MacBook Air sitting on Lydia's lap. "I have a business proposition for you."

"You want to be one of my clients?"

Her aunt nodded.

Lydia glanced around the porch. "Are you thinking of updating the house?"

"No, I'd like you to renovate the old motel on the outskirts of town."

"The Moonlight Motel?" The janky dump had seen its best years five decades ago. "I thought that place had shut down."

"It's still open…when the manager feels like flipping on the vacancy sign." Amelia snorted. "Stampede is falling apart right before my eyes."

Lydia's grandmother had always wished her sister would leave "that godforsaken dusty hideaway for diehard wranglers and has-been cowboys."

"Stampede is losing tourist dollars to our neighbors in Rocky Point and Mesquite all because our mayor isn't willing to put a little money and elbow grease into sprucing up the town."

"Why the motel?"

"It's the only place people can stay when they visit Stampede."

"What shape is the building in?"

"The rooms haven't been updated since the '70s."

"Do you have the approval of the owner to fix it up?"

"I do. And Emmett Hardell's grandson will be helping you."

"Which grandson?"

"Gunner manages the motel when he's not off pretending he's a rodeo cowboy."

Lydia recalled the hot look Gunner had sent her in church during her uncle's funeral. Later that day she'd overheard her mother and Aunt Amelia chatting about the Hardell boys. Her aunt had blamed their wild ways on the lack of a female influence in their lives. The boys' mother had abandoned the family, and then a few years later their grandmother had passed away, leaving their "tomcatting" father and "irritable" grandfather— Aunt Amelia's words—to raise the boys.

"How old is Gunner?"

"A year older than you, I believe."

"As far as renovating the motel," Lydia said, "you're just looking to freshen up the paint colors and change the furniture and decor?"

"That's right. And I'll pay you for your work."

"You don't have to do that, Aunt Amelia."

"Of course I do."

Lydia breathed a sigh of relief, happy she wouldn't have to dig into her dismal savings to cover the bills next month. "I should be able to handle the task."

"I wouldn't have asked you to take on this project if I didn't believe you had the talent and skill to pull it off."

"Let's visit the motel in the morning and come up with a design plan."

"You'll have to go by yourself, dear. I have choir practice after church services."

Lydia had forgotten that tomorrow was Sunday.

"As far as decorating ideas, I'm leaving that in your capable hands."

"What's my budget?"

"There is no budget. Do what needs to be done to

turn the motel into a place people will drive out of their way to spend the night."

"Are you covering the entire bill for this renovation?"

Her aunt nodded. "I've got more money than I know what to do with, Lydia."

That was the truth. Everyone in the family knew that Uncle Robert had left Aunt Amelia millions of dollars in stocks and oil investments. "I don't have many years left on this earth, and before I meet my Maker, I want Stampede to return to its glory days."

Her aunt would have better odds buying lottery tickets because there was no guarantee that all the beautification in the world would bring tourists back to this hidey-hole-in-the-wall.

"How will I get into the motel rooms to take a look around?"

Her aunt reached into the pocket of her slacks and pulled out a key. "This will open the front office and the room keys are hanging on a pegboard behind the counter."

The motel rooms still used keys? "I'll have a better idea of the cost of the makeover once I see the place."

"If the mayor shows up while you're looking around, just ignore him."

"Who's the mayor?"

"I thought you knew."

Lydia shook her head.

"Emmett Hardell is the mayor."

"Grandma claimed you were sweet on Emmett when you were in high school. How come you two didn't end up together?"

"Because the man's dumb as a rock when it comes to women." Amelia waved a hand before her face. "He married my best friend, Sara Pritchett. She was a sweet girl."

Lydia wondered if the mayor had any idea what he was up against, taking on Aunt Amelia. If he didn't, he was about to find out.

Chapter Two

Sunday morning Lydia woke up and stared into her open suitcase. She wanted to make a good first impression with the Moonlight Motel manager—even if he was just a country boy. If she wanted Gunner Hardell to take her seriously, then she'd better dress as a professional. She picked out a black maxi skirt and a short-sleeved white poppy-print blouse, then headed for the shower.

A half hour later with her wet hair secured in a bun at the back of her head, she walked into an empty kitchen. Her aunt had left a note on the table. *Good luck today.* After washing her antibiotic down with a glass of orange juice, she took her bowl of bran flakes outside and ate breakfast on the front porch swing.

Her aunt's home sat on the corner of Buckaroo Avenue and Vaquero Lane. A yellow butterfly vine in full bloom covered the wrought iron fence enclosing the front yard. A large magnolia tree shaded the porch and smaller crepe myrtle trees lined the driveway, their pink blooms scattered across the black asphalt. Boston ferns hung from ornate vintage hooks along the porch overhang and a pot of daisies sat on the table between a pair of white rockers at the end of the porch.

Aunt Amelia took pride in her home and Lydia wasn't surprised that she wanted to tidy up the town. All of her neighbors kept their properties neatly landscaped—even the yard of the home with a for-sale sign out front had been mowed recently.

Lydia swallowed the last bite of cereal and returned inside to brush her teeth and put on lip gloss. With her computer in hand, she grabbed her purse and left the house. She drove through town at a snail's pace—not much had changed since she'd last visited Stampede.

Three blocks of businesses formed Chuck Wagon Drive, the main thoroughfare. The brick buildings dated back to the late 1800s and early 1900s—the National Bank and Trust still remained a bank. The old Woolworth had closed its doors decades ago and now the building housed the Cattle Drive Café on the main floor, the town library in the basement and Statewide Insurance on the third level. The feedstore built circa the 1870s took up an entire block, the doors and windows boarded over. Years of baking in the hot sun had bleached the wood gray. For Sale had been spray-painted on the side of the building.

There were no stop signs in Stampede, just slow signs posted along the side streets. The third block along the main thoroughfare consisted of newer brick storefronts, but the Saddle Up Saloon's window had a huge crack through it and the sign for the Crazy Curl Hair Salon hung crooked. An out-of-business poster had been taped to the window of the Buckets of Suds coin-operated laundry. Right next door a rocking chair and overturned milk can sat in the display window of Millie's Antiques & Resale—Open Saturdays had been painted across the window.

The old Amoco filling station on the corner had been converted into a farmers' market. Empty vegetable and fruit crates littered the back of the lot next to a dilapidated snow-cone stand. The Corner Market sat at the end of the block—Lydia remembered walking there as a kid and buying five-cent candy.

There was no landscaping in front of the businesses, no benches to sit on or flowerpots to admire—nothing but bare sidewalks with weeds growing through the cracks in the cement. No wonder Aunt Amelia was frustrated with the mayor's lack of interest in beautifying the town. Stampede was aptly named—it looked as if a herd of renegade bovines had trampled the life out of it.

After the last block Lydia hit the gas. A half mile up the highway, the sign for Moonlight Motel came into view—a full moon sitting on top of a forty-foot pole. When the sign was turned on, the moon glowed white and spun in a slow circle. No Vacancy was spelled out across the moon, and depending on whether or not the motel was full, the letters in the Vacancy or No Vacancy glowed blue against the white backdrop of the moon.

She pulled into the parking lot of the six-room tan brick motel and parked by the office. Weeds and trash littered the empty lot. A person would have to be desperate for shelter to rent a room here, which played in Lydia's favor. Anything she did to the place would be an improvement.

The motel was shaped like a capital *L*. The rooms were numbered sequentially—starting with 1 next to the office. The once-royal-blue trim and doors had faded to baby blue. There was no pool or recreation area for families to picnic or relax and the office with its peeling window tint gave the impression the place had closed down.

She locked the car door, then used the key her aunt had given her to let herself into the office. The dim interior smelled musty like a suitcase that hadn't been opened in decades. A chair with an inch of dust coating the leather seat sat in the corner next to a table covered in old tourist brochures. She set the key on the counter, then glanced through the leaflets advertising cave tours and shopping outlets.

"If it isn't the dairyland princess."

Lydia spun and came face-to-face with Gunner Hardell.

He removed his cowboy hat. "We bumped into each other at the Valero yesterday."

"We did?"

"You walked right past me without looking my way."

Embarrassed she hadn't noticed him, she said, "I'm sorry. I was in a hurry."

"You grew up real nice, Lydia Canter."

So had Gunner. His grin widened, drawing her eyes to his sexy mouth. *Handsome* wasn't the right word to describe the dark-haired cowboy. H-O-T with a dozen exclamation points fit better. Too bad none of the men on the dating site she'd joined looked like Gunner.

Her attention shifted to his hands. He wasn't wearing a wedding ring.

Gunner cleared his throat and she looked away, mortified that he'd caught her studying him. "I understand you're the manager of the Moonlight Motel."

"I mostly rodeo and do this—" he spread his arms wide "—on the side to keep Gramps happy."

"So you know why I'm here." She tore her gaze from his face and pretended to study her surroundings, irritated that he made her nervous. There weren't any guys like Gunner on SavvyMatch.com. He was too confident and sure of himself to fit the profiles of the socially awkward men who'd been matched up with her.

"If you ask me," he said, "the motel doesn't need a makeover."

Seriously? Maybe a bull had kicked the cowboy in the head and scrambled his brains. "I'd like to peek inside one of the rooms. I assume the motel is empty."

"Then you'd assume wrong."

Her gaze shifted to the front window. "There aren't any cars parked in the lot."

"The couple in room 6 didn't arrive by car." Gunner waggled an eyebrow and a red flag rose inside Lydia's head.

"Did an Uber driver drop them off?"

Gunner laughed, showing off a row of white teeth. She pressed a hand to her belly, thinking she must have swallowed a fly while eating her cereal outside—the winged insect wouldn't stop fluttering inside her stomach.

"Maybelle and Hector rode in on horseback. Red's hitched to the lean-to behind the motel."

There was a lean-to on the property?

"Hector and Maybelle have a standing reservation at the end of every month."

"That means the motel is always open on that weekend?"

"Not if I'm rodeoing," he said. "I had an extra room key made for them."

How trusting of him. "Are you away riding horses often?"

Dark eyebrows slanted toward his nose. "You mean broncs."

"Same difference."

The brows dipped lower. "Not really."

"Have you won any buckles?" She'd learned a few things about rodeo from her trips to Texas to visit Aunt Amelia—only the really talented cowboys won buckles and money.

Gunner straightened his shoulders. "No."

"If you're not any good at rodeo, why do you keep competing at the sport?"

"Beats waiting for someone to rent a room."

"Giving the motel a face-lift will improve your wait times."

"What's up with your aunt wanting to fix this place, anyway?"

"She's hoping it will entice tourists to check out Stampede." Lydia shrugged. "You have to admit the town is depressing."

"I guess your aunt's reasons don't matter. The sooner the property passes her inspection, the sooner I get back to busting broncs."

"And the sooner I can go home." At least they were in agreement on that issue.

"So pick a color and I'll slap a fresh coat of paint on the outside and we'll call it good to go. Maybelle and Hector don't care what the place looks like as long as the sheets are clean."

Lydia would decide when the motel was "good to go." "Will you show me around outside before I take a look at one of the rooms?" She turned on her laptop and opened the interior-design software program.

"What are you doing?"

She used her fingertip to draw on the screen. "Making notes."

"What is it you do for a living that qualifies you for this project?"

"I'm an interior designer."

"Did you go to college?" he asked.

"Yes. Didn't you?"

He shook his head. "College is for people who can't get a real job."

"Well, you can't ride Wisconsin cows—you can only milk them. So I guess it's a good thing you live in Texas and I went to college."

The corner of his mouth quivered, but he kept a straight face. "This way." He grabbed a golf club leaning against the wall and walked through the doorway behind the checkout desk. She followed him down the short hallway and out the back door.

The lot behind the motel consisted of gravel, dirt, weeds and a small grassy field where Red stood in the shade beneath the lean-to. Lydia made a note on her laptop to ask her aunt if there was enough money in the budget to put in a patio and a children's playground. A family-friendly motel might encourage Maybelle and Hector to find another place to rendezvous.

She eyed the Dumpster filled to the top with garbage, broken furniture and an old tire. "When do you have the trash picked up?"

"When it overflows." He walked over to a patch of weeds and swung the club, taking the tops off the dandelions.

She clicked on a new tab and drew a space for an entertainment area. Absorbed in adding details to the sketch, she wasn't aware that Gunner had inched closer until his breath hit the back of her neck. She inhaled sharply and his scent—a combination of woodsy cologne and pure cowboy—shot up her nose. She attempted to move away, but little suction cups had sprouted on the bottoms of her shoes, keeping her rooted in place.

"Hey, that's pretty cool that you can draw like that. What about putting in a barbecue so guests can cook out." He touched his finger against the corner of the screen. "Right here."

"That's a great idea."

"Buy one of those grills with a built-in smoker."

Of course he'd want that. If her aunt's plan failed to bring tourists to Stampede, Gunner and his rodeo buddies would use the patio to barbecue and party.

His masculine finger moved to the opposite corner of the screen and whatever he said next failed to register with her because she was wondering how that calloused finger would feel trailing over her lips or across her cheek or along her… Never mind.

Shocked by the path her thoughts were taking, Lydia closed the laptop. "I'm ready to look at a room."

She followed him back to the office, where he grabbed the key to room 3 from the pegboard behind the check-in desk. She held out her hand. "You don't have to come with me."

He stared into her eyes as if he could read her thoughts and knew he made her nervous. "You sure?"

"Very." Key in hand, she left the office, sucking in a deep breath of dusty air, hoping the gritty particles would clear Gunner's scent from her head. She didn't condone his lackadaisical management style, but at least when he was off rodeoing, his sexy pheromones wouldn't interfere with her work.

Good grief. Not in a millions years would she have thought she'd be attracted to a slacker.

A LOUD CHUGGING NOISE woke Gunner and he popped out of the chair in the motel office, where he'd fallen asleep after Lydia had gone off to explore room 3. He peered out the window. What the heck was his grandfather doing here?

He stepped outside and waited for the old 1970 Ford to pull into a parking spot. "I thought you were helping Logan feed the cattle this morning," he said when the driver-side door opened.

"Too hot." His grandfather took the pack of Marlboro from his shirt pocket and lit up. "Thanks for the birthday smokes."

Gunner had left a happy-birthday note on the kitchen table along with the cigarettes and the snake, which he'd wrapped in newspaper. "You weren't supposed to open your gifts until supper."

"You wasted your money on that stupid snake. Should have bought another pack of cigarettes."

"The snake was cheaper."

His grandfather's mouth twitched.

"Since it's your birthday, you should go fishing at the lake."

"I might later." He tilted his head toward the office. "I wasn't sure you'd show up today."

"I got your message loud and clear. I'm at Lydia's beck 'n' call until this place sparkles and shines."

His grandfather fussed with his belt, then smoothed a hand over his head. Gunner couldn't remember the last time the old man had taken a comb to his hair, but this morning he'd slicked it down with enough Brylcreem to suffocate a beehive. "Is that a new shirt you're wearing?"

"No." His grandfather's gaze slid sideways.

The creases from the package were still visible. And was that Hai Karate cologne he smelled?

"Did Amelia come with Lydia?"

Before Gunner answered the question, the self-appointed matriarch of Stampede drove her white 1958 Thunderbird convertible into the parking lot. For an instant he envisioned Lydia behind the wheel of the sexy piece of machinery, her blond hair flying in the wind.

His grandfather dropped his cigarette on the ground and stomped it out with his boot heel—a boot that had been spit-shined and polished. *Well, well, well.* That explained the Brylcreem and the cologne. Why his grandfather wanted to impress Amelia Rinehart was a mystery when all they ever did was spar with each other.

Amelia parked next to Emmett's pickup and Gunner rushed over to open the door and help her out of the front seat. "'Morning, Ms. Amelia."

"Hello, Gunner." She peeked around his shoulder. "Emmett."

"Amelia."

Gunner shut the door, his gaze shifting between the older couple. "Happy birthday," Amelia said.

"I don't much care for birthdays anymore."

She smiled. "Who does at our age?"

His grandfather's gaze rolled over Amelia like a

teenage boy and Gunner looked away, embarrassed by his grandfather's gawking.

"Where's Lydia?" Amelia asked.

"Inspecting room 3," Gunner said.

His grandfather elbowed him in the ribs. "You should be showing her around in case she has questions."

"Why would she have any questions? Everything in the rooms has to go."

Oh, man. The old lady was going to pick a fight with his grandfather.

"Vintage is all the rage," she said. "But those brown bedspreads weren't brown when they were first put on the beds."

"Nothing wrong with covers that hide dirt," Emmett said.

"Dirt and the infestation of every imaginable bug."

The door to room 6 opened and Hector and Maybelle waltzed outside—Maybelle still buttoning her blouse. The couple froze when they noticed their audience.

Gunner waved. "Safe travels!"

"Who's that?" Amelia asked.

"Hector Montoya. He works at the Los Lobos Ranch." The spread butted up to the Hardell ranch and they raised cattle and alpaca—not wolves like the name implied. "Maybelle's the ranch maid."

"For Pete's sake," Amelia said, "Why don't they get married instead of sneaking around?" The couple disappeared behind the motel.

"Marriage isn't for everyone," Emmett grumbled.

Gunner agreed. His grandfather still grieved the passing of his wife. Emmett might be a grumpy old man, but he showed his love for others in unique ways—like buying the Moonlight Motel for Sara after she'd been diagnosed with cancer. Gunner's grand-mother had dreamed of running the motel and Gunner figured his grandfather had hoped the place would lift her spirits and encourage her to fight the disease, but Emmett's plan hadn't worked out like he'd intended.

"What are you charging for a room these days, Gunner?" Amelia asked.

"It varies," he said.

"You don't have a set rate?"

"I charge whatever the person can afford to pay me."

Amelia's gaze swung to Emmett. "No wonder you've never been able to pay back—"

"I'm done jawing about this place." Emmett walked over to the truck. "Gunner."

"Yes, sir?"

"You stick to the plan, you hear?"

"I will."

"Hold up." Amelia thrust out her arm, preventing Emmett from closing the truck door.

Gunner held his breath, worried his grandfather would say something he couldn't take back, which was how he ended most arguments.

"What's this about a plan? You're not interfering with—"

"I told Gunner to keep an eye on your niece to make sure she doesn't ruin the place."

"What utter nonsense. Lydia doesn't need a baby-sitter." Amelia looked at Gunner. "No offense, young man, but my niece has a degree in interior design. In fact, she has her own design company. She's more than capable of handling a motel makeover."

"Just the same," Emmett said, "Gunner's keeping

an eye on things so the place doesn't get turned into a pink palace."

"A pink palace would be better—" Amelia spread her arms wide "—than a motel that looks like it belongs in an Alfred Hitchcock movie."

"Keep the place rustic. This is cowboy country and there aren't any fancy-pants oilmen living around these parts anymore."

Amelia's eyes flashed with anger. "You never did approve of Robert and he had nothing but nice things to say about you."

Why had his grandfather brought up Amelia's deceased husband? Gunner had better intervene before the conversation went too far south. "Time-out, folks."

They ignored him, their eyes locked in a death stare. The door to room 3 opened and Lydia stepped into view. "There's the designer," Gunner said, hoping her presence would calm the bickering duo.

"What's going on?" Lydia's worried gaze took in the scene. "I thought you had choir practice after church, Aunt Amelia."

"We ended early," Amelia said.

Gunner scowled at his grandfather, warning him to keep his mouth shut.

Lydia tugged on Gunner's shirtsleeve. "What did I miss?"

"They were discussing the renovations," Gunner said.

"I took enough notes to begin designing," Lydia said.

"How long will it take to get the job done?" Gunner asked.

"Once I line up the contractors, only a few weeks."

"There's your contractor." Emmett pointed to Gunner.

"Besides rodeoing, you work in the trades, too?" Lydia asked.

"My grandson doesn't work at much of anything, but he's agreed to sit out a few rodeos and help you." Emmett returned Gunner's evil-eyed glare.

"It's best to hire professionals—"

"I've snaked my share of pipes." Gunner interrupted Lydia. "And it doesn't take much talent to roll paint on a wall."

"Gunner's in charge of the place," Emmett said, climbing into his truck. "He's got the final say on how things get done."

Amelia scoffed. "Being mayor has gone to your head."

"I know what's best for this town."

"If we don't do something drastic to turn things around, Stampede will only be home to you and a handful of ghosts."

His grandfather closed the door and leaned his head out the open window. "I'd rather this place become a ghost town than have a bunch of strangers and hooligans roaming the streets."

"There's only one street and your grandsons were the last bunch of ruffians to run wild around here. There's been no vandalism since—" Amelia nodded to Gunner "—he spray-painted images of bare-breasted women on the back of the Woolworth building."

Lydia smiled. "Maybe Gunner would like to paint a mural on the wall outside the motel office."

Gunner dragged a hand over his face. He'd never live down that bad decision. The two geriatrics continued bickering like kids fighting in a sandbox and he worried one of them might suffer a stroke.

"You don't know when to leave well enough alone, Amelia." Emmett turned the key in the ignition. When the engine backfired, the two women jumped inside their skin.

Amelia shook her fist in Emmett's face. "You used to be fun. Now you're just a grumpy old man."

When had his grandfather ever been fun?

Emmett put the truck in Reverse and Amelia stomped back to her car. She started to back out of her spot but slammed on the brakes when Emmett cut her off. She laid on the horn. Emmett waved her to go first. She waved back at him. After two false starts and stops, Amelia headed for the highway, Emmett's pickup inches from her bumper. Then she slammed on her brakes at the entrance and Emmett swerved in order to miss hitting her car.

He stuck his head out the window and shouted, "It's Sunday! What are you waiting for? Monday?"

Amelia turned left onto the highway and headed toward town. Emmett turned right and headed away from town. After the vehicles disappeared from sight, Gunner said, "What the hell just happened?"

"I have no idea."

He opened his mouth to ask about the plans Lydia had drawn on her computer when Hector and Maybelle rode into view on Red. Hector stopped the horse in front of Gunner and held out a twenty-dollar bill, then turned Red east and rode off.

"Gunner?"

"What?"

"I appreciate the offer, but I won't be needing your help with the renovations."

"I know."

"So you'll stay out of the way and let me do my job?"

Lydia looked so hopeful that he almost caved in. "Sorry. You're stuck with me."

"I was afraid you'd say that."

"When do we start?" he asked.

"As soon as I come up with a design my aunt likes." She walked to her car and retrieved her cell phone from her purse. "Give me your number."

He recited the digits and she entered them into her phone. "Are all of the rooms set up the same as number 3?"

"Yep."

"I'll be in touch shortly." She got into her car and drove off.

Gunner stood in the empty parking lot long after the Civic disappeared. The dairyland princess wasn't his usual type, but her presence around the motel was bound to liven things up.

Chapter Three

"Aunt Amelia, you need to choose a design." Lydia smiled even though she felt like throwing a temper tantrum. Three days had gone by since she'd toured the Moonlight Motel this past Sunday and had taken extensive notes on the property. She'd spent Monday creating two different designs for the makeover, and when her aunt wasn't happy with either, she'd come up with a third idea. She didn't have all summer to work on the motel, so today she was determined to move forward with the renovations.

"I'm not sure which one I like best," Amelia said.

"Let's go over them again." *For the hundredth time.* Lydia joined her aunt at the kitchen table and opened the laptop. "This is the more expensive renovation, which includes a patio and playground behind the motel."

"I like the idea of families being able to use the grill and children having a place to play."

"A playground is cheaper to maintain than a pool and can be used all year round," Lydia said.

Her aunt studied the first design. "It's beautiful, tasteful, the colors are lovely, but…"

"What?"

"Maybe a little too cosmopolitan."

Lydia clenched her hands beneath the table. "You said you wanted to bring this dusty cowboy town into the twenty-first century."

"I do, but Emmett has a point. This is Hill Country. Tourists will want the Texas experience when they stay at the motel and this room looks like it belongs in Chicago or New York City."

Until now Lydia had avoided discussing the strained conversation between her aunt and Emmett at the motel. "What's going on between you and Gunner's grandfather?"

Amelia's eyes widened before she dropped her gaze and picked at a piece of lint on her slacks. "Nothing. Why?"

"You mentioned that you dated Emmett in high school, but he married your friend Sara."

Her aunt's eyes glazed over and she stared into space. "It's probably difficult to imagine, but that man was such a tease back in the day."

"You were partial to cowboys then?" Lydia asked.

Amelia nodded. "Weekends he worked alongside his father at the Triple D. They lived on the property and his mother cooked and cleaned for the Masterson family."

"How'd Emmett end up owning his own ranch?"

"I was twenty-five when Baron Masterson passed away and his wife sold the ranch off in parcels. Emmett's father was a frugal man and had saved enough money to buy one of the tracts."

"What about your father? Why didn't he purchase any land?"

"My father was ten years older than Emmett's and

he was 'tired of chasing cows'—his words not mine."
Amelia smiled. "He hung up his spurs and Mother's
paycheck was enough to keep the two of them afloat.
Robert and I helped them make ends meet when my
mother eventually retired from the bank."

"How many kids did Emmett and Sara have?"

"Just Gunner's father, Donny. He died almost a year
to the day after Robert's funeral."

"What happened?"

"Donny was changing a flat tire on the side of the
road at night and was struck by a passing motorist.
They never did find the person who hit him."

"That's awful."

"It was hard on the three boys. Their mother had left
the family years earlier and then they lost their grandmother after that. When Donny died, Emmett fell off
the wagon and began drinking again."

"I didn't know he was an alcoholic."

"Donny was a drinker, too."

Lydia hoped Gunner hadn't followed in his father's
footsteps. The last thing she needed was an inebriated
handyman helping her renovate the motel.

"When Emmett's drinking got out of hand, Logan
quit rodeoing and came home. It wasn't long after that
Emmett gave up booze, but by then he'd lost interest
in Paradise Ranch and had handed the reins over to
Logan."

"Sounds like Gunner had a challenging childhood."

"Don't feel too sorry for that young man. It's time
he grew up and ran that motel the right way."

Lydia had a hundred more questions about Gunner
but didn't want to give her aunt the impression she was
interested in him, which she wasn't. Even if she were,

according to SavvyMatch.com, he wasn't a good pick for her. "We're getting sidetracked. You said that you wanted to bring Stampede back to its glory days. What about Western-themed rooms? Cowboys, ranching and cattle." Personally, Lydia thought that kind of decor was cheesy. But… "People staying at the motel would experience a taste of the old Wild West."

"You might be onto something," Amelia said. "The motel has to be special to convince people to drive out of their way to spend a night."

Lydia tapped her finger against the tabletop, her mind racing through the images she'd committed to memory from the gazillion decorating magazines she'd subscribed to. *Bingo!* "What if each room showcased a Western movie from a different decade?"

Her aunt clapped her hands. "Emmett would love the idea and Rocky Point and Mesquite don't have any motels like that."

"I'll see what I can come up with." Lydia slid the laptop into her leather messenger bag.

"Where are you going?" Amelia asked.

"To the library to do research."

"In an hour I'm meeting with the Stampede Chamber of Commerce to discuss other ideas for the town."

Lydia hoped her design skills weren't needed for those plans or she'd be stuck in Stampede forever. "I'll see you later." She drove over to the old Woolworth building and parked in the lot. She studied the back of the structure but couldn't find any trace of Gunner's graffiti drawing from years ago. The smell of fried eggs and sausage from the Cattle Drive Café followed her down the flight of stairs to the basement.

The librarian's desk sat empty when Lydia walked

into the room, so she wandered around, searching for books, magazines or journals that would inspire decorating ideas. After striking out, she connected the laptop to the free Wi-Fi and began Googling. Two hours later and suffering from information overload, she took a break to check her email.

Lydia was in between projects after finishing a redesign of a loft apartment for a newlywed couple in downtown Madison. She'd submitted ideas for a bedroom makeover to Mrs. Higginson two weeks ago but hadn't heard back. She sent the woman a follow-up email asking if she had any questions or concerns about the ideas, then logged in to SavvyMatch.com—a dating site "for practical people looking for the perfect match."

While the site loaded, she thought of Gunner. Her gut insisted there wasn't an ounce of practical in his DNA. Men like Gunner were so far off her radar they might as well live on the moon. Lydia was searching for a guy who wanted the same things she did. A home in the suburbs, a minivan and at least two kids—because she'd hated being an only child.

Her profile popped up with three heart icons next to her photo. She clicked on the first heart and Jonathan001 appeared on the screen. He was thirty-four. A construction engineer—his profession complemented hers more than a bronc-busting cowboy's did. Jonathan had never been married. He lived in Middleton—a suburb of Madison. His hobbies included bicycling, hiking and golf. So far the man was batting a hundred. She pictured Gunner wearing spandex biking shorts and a cowboy hat, and then her imagination switched out the shorts for a pair of salmon-colored golf pants—no way would Gunner be caught dead wearing the outfits.

Jonathan had a nice smile, but she wished he'd taken off the riding helmet he wore in his picture so she could see if he was hiding a receding hairline. Gunner had a thick head of shaggy hair in need of a trim. Lydia's gaze zeroed in on the front of Jonathan's spandex shorts—Mother Nature hadn't left him well endowed. Gunner probably had more than he knew what to do with.

Before she opened the second heart icon on her profile page, her stomach gurgled with hunger. She sniffed the air and caught the smell of grilled hamburgers and frying bacon. She checked the time on her phone and was surprised she'd been at the library almost three hours. She collected her things and returned upstairs to the café.

"Seat yourself, honey!" the waitress called out.

Lydia slid into a booth and perused the laminated menu.

"Name's Dolly. You passing through town or here visiting someone?" The redhead placed a glass of water on the table.

"Visiting. I'm Lydia Canter." She offered her hand. "Amelia Rinehart is my great-aunt."

"Well, I'll be. Welcome to Stampede."

"Thank you."

"Bart's in the kitchen today and he can't cook a decent hamburger if his life depended on it. If I were you, I'd order a grilled cheese."

"That sounds good, thanks."

"Can I get you anything else to drink?"

"Water is fine."

"Be back in a jiffy."

Lydia opened her laptop, pulled up the dating site

again and studied Jonathan's image. She considered the men her college girlfriends had married and none of them were sex gods. They were good, decent, caring guys and Lydia needed to keep that in mind when she perused the profiles. She wanted to be attracted to the man she married, but more important, she wanted him to stick by her side through good times and bad.

"If I'd known you were into spandex, I'd have worn tights today."

Lydia glanced over her shoulder, her head almost bumping into Gunner's nose. How long had he been peeking over her shoulder?

He sat across from her in the booth. "Is that the type of guy who turns you on?"

"If you mean educated and mature, then yes."

"You can do better."

"Really?" She clicked on the second heart icon and spun the computer toward him. "What about this one?"

Gunner studied the photo, then shook his head. "Nope."

"I thought for sure he'd pass inspection because he's wearing jeans."

"You need—"

"I'm not interested in your dating advice."

"You should be. I have a lot of experience in picking out top-of-the-line models."

"By *top-of-the-line* I'm sure you mean brainless."

"The ladies I court don't need brains. They have other assets that endear them to me."

Lydia scoffed. "You're afraid of intelligent, independent women, aren't you?"

"I'd love to date a beauty with brains, but those women are too demanding."

"And you're Mr. Laid-Back?"

"Life's too short to be serious all the time." He pointed at her. "Take you for example. You have work-aholic written all over you."

"I own a business. I have to work hard to stay afloat."

"I thought your parents were wealthy. Aren't they lawyers or judges or something?"

"Lawyers, and just because they make a comfort-able living, doesn't mean they want to support their grown daughter forever."

"Since you're busy with your—" he nodded to the laptop "—dating business right now—" he flashed a grin "—let's hold off on the renovations. There's a rodeo I'd like to enter this weekend."

"There's plenty to do around the property to pre-pare for the remodel."

"Like what?"

"Empty the Dumpster in the back and arrange to donate the furniture in the rooms to a charity."

"That's a couple of phone calls. Consider that done today." He waved his hand. "What else?"

His boyish smile messed with her train of thought and she couldn't recall what else was on her to-do list, so she changed the subject. "I doubt you're interested, but we've got a theme for the motel."

"A theme?"

"Each room will represent a Western movie."

"That sounds stupid."

"I was hoping you'd say that."

"You were?"

She smiled. "If you think it's ridiculous, then I know it's a great idea."

"WELL?" LYDIA WRUNG her hands as she waited for her aunt's opinion Saturday morning. After she'd run into Gunner at the café in town on Wednesday, she'd spent the rest of the week tweaking her designs.

"Movie-themed rooms." Amelia adjusted her glasses and peered at the laptop screen on the kitchen table. "I like that you chose old Westerns."

Lydia had selected six movies from different decades and each with a different leading male actor. "Do you think Gunner's grandfather will approve?"

"Emmett's a big John Wayne fan. He'll love the *Stagecoach* room."

Lydia stopped pacing. "Good."

"How will people know what movie the room represents?" Amelia asked.

"Instead of numbers on the room doors, we'll use placards with the movie title. Number 6 will be called the Stagecoach Room."

Amelia nodded. "And the others will be the San Antonio with Errol Flynn, High Noon with Gary Cooper, Once Upon a Time in the West with Henry Fonda, McCabe and Mrs. Miller with Warren Beatty and Unforgiven with Clint Eastwood."

Lydia tapped the laptop screen and another design folder opened. "There's a business that creates custom wallpapers. I'll pick a famous scene with the main actor from each movie and put that wallpaper behind the beds."

"I love it."

"I'll head over to the motel to take measurements and put the finishing touches on these designs." Lydia packed up her laptop.

"I'm going to Boerne with Margaret for her granddaughter's baby shower." Amelia placed an extra house key on the table. "We're staying overnight at the William Hotel, then having breakfast with Margaret's granddaughter in the morning before we do a little shopping."

"Sounds nice." Lydia dropped the key into her purse. "Who's driving?"

Her aunt arched an eyebrow. "Are you worried I can't navigate the roads anymore?"

"I didn't mean to offend you, Aunt Amelia."

"You didn't, dear. Margaret's driving, and before you ask, she's fifty-six."

"Don't forget your cell phone in case I need to get in touch with you about the motel." Lydia kissed her aunt's cheek. "I'll see you tomorrow night." She paused at the back door. "If you find any John Wayne souvenirs, buy them for the Stagecoach Room." It was eight thirty when Lydia left her aunt's home and the only business open at that hour in Stampede was the café. Hopefully Gunner was awake and already at work.

When she pulled into the motel, she caught a glimpse of the empty Dumpster at the back of the property. Gunner had followed through on his promise to have the trash hauled away. Maybe he was the kind of guy who just needed to be told what to do. Lydia got out of the car, but her steps slowed as she approached the office, where a note had been taped to the door. *Got a ride in Rocky Point.* Her handyman had ditched her. Lydia dug around inside her purse, searching for the motel office key her aunt had given her when she'd first arrived in town. When her fingers came up empty, she remembered she'd placed the key on the counter inside the office when she'd toured the motel this past Sunday.

Frustrated, she called Gunner's cell. No answer. Next she tested the knob on each room door, thinking he might have left one of them open. They were all locked.

Lydia was aware that Gunner and his grandfather weren't keen on the motel makeover, but they weren't calling the shots—her aunt was. She hopped into the Civic and turned on her GPS app, then spoke into the phone.

"Directions to Rocky Point, Texas."

Twenty-eight minutes later, Lydia reached the outskirts of the town. She followed the signs to the fairgrounds, which were hardly impressive. The area looked as if a field of scrub brush had been plowed under and a fence thrown up around a dirt circle. A pair of aluminum bleachers sat outside the makeshift arena. There was no concession stand—just his and her porta-potties located next to the livestock pens.

She parked between a Ford and a Dodge pickup, then grabbed her purse and headed for the entrance, where a bowlegged cowboy wearing a money belt stood guard. "Ten dollars, missy."

"You're charging to watch the rodeo?"

"How else are the boys gonna get paid?" He rubbed a gray-whiskered cheek. "You ain't from around here, are ya?"

"No, sir." She handed him two five-dollar bills. "Where are the cowboys?"

He nodded to the single bucking chute, where a group of men had gathered. As if the geezer read her mind, he said, "Spectators ain't allowed over there."

"How long does the rodeo last?"

"Couple of hours. Give or take."

Sitting on bleachers in the hot sun for two hours watching grown men tussle with crazed livestock hadn't been on Lydia's to-do list today. At least the makeup she wore had sunscreen in it. "Do you have a program?"

He shook his head. "Bob's on the mike today. He'll tell ya a bit about the boys before they ride."

Lydia climbed the bleachers and sat behind a pair of buckle bunnies. The women flashed their bold painted lips at her and she returned their smiles. The brunette's gaze caught on Lydia's navy linen slacks, reminding her that she looked out of place among all the denim and cowboy boots.

A cowboy walked in front of the stands and the dark-haired woman waved her arms wildly, her hat falling onto Lydia's lap.

"Sorry," the cowgirl said, snatching it back. The white Stetson matched the woman's white shirt covered with pink rhinestones. The platinum blonde next to her wore a black shirt covered in silver rhinestones and Lydia suspected the cowgirls owned a BeDazzler machine.

Small-town girls in Wisconsin joined their local 4-H and dressed for wrangling milking cows and sheep, not rodeo cowboys.

"Wanna bet he'll be last, Maisy?" The brunette spoke to her friend.

"Has Gunner asked you out yet?" Maisy asked.

Lydia's ears perked when she heard the motel manager's name.

"No, but he will."

"That cowboy will never let a woman rein him in, Chantilly."

Chantilly?

"Gunner says he's a confirmed bachelor, but I'll change his mind."

Oh, brother. The women made Gunner sound like some kind of cowboy god. Then again, Lydia conceded the man was better looking than any of the guys who'd pinged her profile on the dating site.

"Ladies and gents, welcome to the fifteenth annual Rocky Point Rodeo." Announcer Bob cleared his throat, then continued in a monotone voice better suited for a PBS broadcast. "Up first is the saddle-bronc competition." The handful of spectators in the stands applauded.

Lydia turned her attention to the bucking chute, searching for Gunner among the milling cowboys. The men were dressed the same—jeans, dark shirts and hats pulled low over their faces. She couldn't tell them apart.

"There he is." Maisy pointed to a lone cowboy. "Gunner's putting on his spurs."

Lydia's gaze latched onto him.

"We've got five cowboys ready to tame broncs today, so let's get on with the show." The applause died down. "First out of the chute on Storm Chaser is John Pennington. This cowboy hails from New Mexico and he's new to the circuit. Let's see if he can make it to the buzzer."

Lydia had been to a rodeo as a kid but hadn't paid attention to the events. She'd been more interested in the clowns who jumped in and out of the barrels. There were no clowns at this rodeo, only cowboys who stood inside the arena near the chute ready to help if needed.

The gate opened and Storm Chaser bolted into the

dirt circle. Cowboy John lasted one buck before sliding off the back end of the horse and landing on the ground.

"Looks like Pennington is gonna need a little more practice before he makes it to eight."

Three more rides followed—resulting in the same outcome. The fans grew restless and the applause disappeared until Gunner stepped up to the chute.

"Our final contestant late this morning lives down the road in Stampede. Gunner Hardell doesn't have any wins on his résumé. Let's see if he shows Spin Demon a thing or two. This bronc is from the Shady Acres Ranch outside of Midland."

Lydia leaned forward, her gaze glued to the chute as Spin Demon sprang into action. Gunner gripped the rope with his left hand, keeping his right arm high in the air next to his head. After the third buck his hat flew off and his dark hair whipped around his head.

Spin Demon did everything in his power to toss his rider and Lydia marveled at Gunner's pure athleticism as he hung on. *Go, Gunner, go.* When the buzzer sounded, she stuck two fingers into her mouth and let loose a shrill whistle.

Chantilly and Maisy spun on their bench, but Lydia ignored their stares and watched Gunner's dismount— more of a fall than a leap to the ground. The bronc trotted out of the circle and Gunner swiped his hat off the dirt, then waved it at the stands. His smile froze when he spotted Lydia.

"Looks like Gunner Hardell finally made it to eight. How about another round of applause for the cowboy."

Instead of returning to the chute area, Gunner walked across the dirt and stopped in front of the bleachers.

"Lydia!" he shouted and then flung his hat. She snatched it as it sailed between Chantilly and Maisy's heads.

"Nice catch." He winked, then walked back to the chutes, where the other cowboys congratulated him with backslapping and fist pumping.

"Who are you?" Chantilly asked.

"Lydia Canter." She beamed, proud of herself for catching Gunner's hat—not that she cared about impressing the women.

"We've never seen you at a rodeo before," Maisy said.

"I'm visiting from Wisconsin."

"Wisconsin?" Chantilly grimaced. "How do you know Gunner?"

"He works for me."

"Doing what?" Maisy asked.

"Anything I ask him to." She pressed her lips together to keep from laughing when their mouths dropped open. "If you'll excuse me, I need to have a chat with my employee."

Lydia pulled up short when a tall, brawny man stepped into her path.

"Ma'am, you ain't allowed behind the chutes."

"She's with me, Rawlins." Gunner strolled toward Lydia, wearing his usual grin. It was impossible to stay mad at a man who smiled all the time.

"Congratulations." She handed him the Stetson.

He plopped it on his head. "Thanks." He removed his spurs, then stuffed them into the duffel bag along with his rope and bronc saddle. "Didn't expect to see you here."

"This isn't my first rodeo, cowboy." He didn't need to know it had been eons since she'd attended one.

"Maybe I pegged you wrong."

"How did you peg me?"

"Boring. All work and no play."

Ouch. A couple of cowboys wandered closer to eavesdrop on their conversation. "Is there somewhere we can talk in private?"

"About what?"

"The motel."

"It's Saturday."

"So?"

"It's the weekend." When she stared at him, he said, "You know, the two days a week most people don't work."

"And the same two days tourists travel and book rooms in motels."

"Not the Moonlight Motel."

"Maybe if the Vacancy sign was turned on, you'd get a few customers."

"Why are you here, Lydia?"

"You locked me out of the motel."

"What happened to your key?" he asked.

She watched a cowboy climb onto a bull in the chute. "I think I left it on the counter Sunday when I stopped by the motel."

"So I didn't really lock you out, then," he said.

Touché.

"What do you say we grab a bite to eat?" he asked.

She held out her hand. "How about you give me the key, and I'll return to the motel and do my job?"

His smile vanished, then slid back into place when Maisy and Chantilly approached them.

"Hey, Gunner." Chantilly batted her eyelashes. "Nice ride."

"You looked real good out there," Maisy added.

"Thank you, ladies."

Ladies? That was a bit of a stretch.

"We're driving over to the Singing Swine." Chantilly inched closer to Gunner. "You up for beer and karaoke?"

Lydia spoke without thinking. "Gunner and I were just about to head there to celebrate his win."

"I don't think the Singing Swine is your kind of place," Maisy said.

She expected Gunner to come to her rescue, but he just stood there grinning. "I'm sure it'll be fine."

Maisy shrugged. "Suit yourself."

After the pair walked off, Gunner spoke. "When was the last time you were in a bar?"

"A month ago," she fibbed. "For a friend's birthday." She'd ordered a glass of wine at TGI Fridays.

"I'll meet you there," he said. "The bar's a mile west of town. Look for the pole with a spinning pink pig."

Spinning pig? Why had she allowed Maisy and Chantilly to provoke her? Lydia shouldn't be wasting her time in some bar. The sooner she began the motel renovations, the sooner she could return to Wisconsin and focus on her design business and finding Mr. Perfect.

Chapter Four

"I'll be damned." Gunner had thought for sure that Lydia would change her mind about meeting him at the Singing Swine, but her blue Civic stood out like a sore thumb among all the pickups in the lot. He parked next to her car, then caught himself checking his reflection in the rearview mirror. He brushed a smudge of dirt from his cheek and reached into the glove compartment for the stick of deodorant and bottle of aftershave he kept for emergencies.

If there had been any other woman waiting inside for him, he would have skipped sprucing up and gone into the bar smelling like a hardworking cowboy. But Lydia Canter was a different breed of lady from his usual hookups and for some stupid reason he cared about her opinion of him.

When he walked inside, he paused until his eyes adjusted to the dim interior. The place wasn't crowded and he found Lydia alone at the bar, chatting with Zeke—the bald bartender with more tattoos than Route 66 had road signs. Gunner was halfway across the room when Lydia tilted her head back and laughed. The sound of her throaty chuckle sent his thoughts racing into the bedroom.

He shook off the image of him and Lydia messing up the sheets and slid onto the empty stool next to her. He nodded to her water glass.

"Why am I not surprised you don't drink?"

"Actually, I love a good glass of red wine, but I'm taking an antibiotic for a sinus infection right now."

Zeke set a longneck in front of Gunner. "Thanks for calling both games Thursday night."

"Anyone heard how long Bill's going to be out?"

"Doc predicted four weeks," Zeke said.

"That hernia pull must have been worse than anyone thought." Gunner looked at Lydia. "I umpire Little League baseball and Bill's our first-base ump." Gunner took a swig of beer. "Kevin had a great hit to center field."

"We've been going to the batting cages in Mesquite," Zeke said.

"Do you need me to call an extra game next week?"

"We've got a sub for Tuesday's game, but I'll let you know if we need you the following week." Zeke moved off to fill another drink order.

"What?" Gunner asked when Lydia continued to stare at him.

"I'm just surprised a guy like you would take the time to help teenagers."

"What do you mean, a guy like me?"

"You said you only care about having a good time."

"That's not all I care about. I love baseball. I played Little League when I was a kid."

"Okay, so you like being around boys who play baseball, but you don't want kids yourself."

Gunner shook his head. "Nope."

"Doesn't make sense," she said.

"Sure it does. I get to have fun with other people's kids, but I don't have to raise them." Gunner took a swig of beer. "What do you think of the Singing Swine?"

"The pig on the pole outside is unique." Her gaze dropped to his waist, then returned to his face. "Did you get a buckle for winning today?"

"Rocky Point doesn't hand out buckles." He didn't care about the hardware—he was just glad to have an excuse not to have to sit at the motel all day and watch cars drive by on the highway.

"How much money did you win?" she asked.

"Enough to fill the gas tank."

"I honestly don't see what all the hype is about," she said. "If it's the adrenaline rush you're after, there are others ways to achieve that without risking injury."

Sex gave him an adrenaline rush, but he doubted that was what Lydia was referring to. "What do you do for kicks?"

She sipped her water, drawing his attention to her mouth. "I like to browse flea markets and vintage shops when I'm not working, which isn't often."

"It sounds like you work too much."

"It's called being an adult."

"Adults are entitled to have fun."

"Agreed," she said. "But keeping up with your responsibilities doesn't leave much time to goof off."

"You're envious of me, aren't you?" he said.

Her mouth dropped open and he tapped his finger beneath her chin until her jaw closed. "I bet your computer is the first thing you check when you wake up and the last thing before you go to sleep." He moved his hand away from her face.

"What's the last thing you look at?" she asked.

"If it's not a woman's face, then it's the TV." He leaned closer. "Wouldn't you rather stare at a pair of brown eyes in the morning instead of a computer screen?"

"You certainly have a healthy ego."

"When's the last time you woke up with a man in your bed?"

She choked on a sip of water and coughed into her napkin. "That's your pickup line?"

He took a swig of beer. "If I was trying to pick you up…what would your comeback be?"

"I don't date freeloaders."

She made him sound like a teenager, not an adult. He could fix that impression by showing her the part of him that was feeling anything but adolescent. "I get it now."

"Get what?"

"Why you had to join a dating site."

Her eyes narrowed. "Why's that?"

"It's not because you aren't pretty enough or sexy enough to find a man on your own, that's for sure."

"You think I'm sexy?"

He thought she was *a lot* sexy, but he played it cool. "You need to show a guy you know how to have fun."

"I don't have time for fun. I'm busy keeping my business afloat. Besides, I'm twenty-six. I'm not about to date a man whose only goal in life is to have a good time. I'd like to marry and have a family."

"Why the rush?"

"My college friends are all married now and three of them have had a baby already. I've always wanted to be a mother."

Babies. Gunner shook his head. Squalling infants

were expensive and a lot of work. He'd listened to the married cowboys on the circuit complain that when they returned home from the road, all they wanted was to rest their injuries and spend long hours in the bedroom with their wives. Most had to settle for a nap while the kids watched TV and a quickie with the wife before one of the babies needed to be fed.

"If I let myself have fun and forget about the future—" she rolled her eyes "—I'll wake up forty and still single."

"That's my plan," he said.

"Are your brothers married?" she asked.

"Logan was, but he and his wife divorced. Reid's never been married—at least, I don't think he has."

"You don't know if your brother ever married or not?"

"Reid hasn't come home since he got out of the military."

"Why?"

"He took our father's death pretty hard and my best guess is that the ranch reminds him of our dad, so he stays away."

"I'm sorry about your father. Aunt Amelia said he was struck by a car."

"Yeah. Gramps fell apart." Gunner and his brothers felt bad, but none of them had been close to their father.

"He's lucky you and your brothers were there for him."

"What about you? Any siblings?"

She shook her head. "I'm an only child."

"That explains why you're so serious. You had to entertain yourself. You didn't have any siblings to get into trouble with." Gunner stared into her eyes. "I bet I know why you're having a problem finding the right guy."

"Really?" She fussed with the collar of her blouse, then smoothed a hand down her slacks.

"If I was on a dating site and came across your profile, I'd think—" he ticked off his fingers "—she's pretty. And she's probably pretty smart if she's running her own business."

"But…?"

He dropped his hand. "You didn't list any fun facts about yourself or what your hobbies are."

"How long were you looking over my shoulder at the Cattle Drive Café?"

"A few minutes."

She jutted her chin. "I have hobbies."

"Name one."

"I like to read."

"What do you read?"

"Design magazines."

"That's for work, not pleasure."

"Maybe if you read a how-to-run-a-motel magazine, you'd have more customers paying to spend the night there," she said.

"You might be right." He tapped the neck of his bottle against her water glass, then drained the contents.

"It's not easy finding a perfect match."

"A perfect match?" He grimaced. "That only happens in movies and books."

"Maybe, but I want to get as close to perfect as possible. I want to be with a man who works as hard as I do. It's expensive raising kids these days. I've watched my cousin Sadie struggle to make ends meet when her sons' father misses one of his child-support payments."

"Money won't make you happy." When his mother had walked out on their family, the Paradise Ranch had been running in the black. But no amount of money or level of financial security could make up for a drunken, cheating husband.

"Having enough money to pay bills removes a lot of stress from a marriage," she said. "Both my parents work and I can't even remember a time when they argued over anything but a legal case."

"So you want what your parents have?"

"They've been happily married for over thirty years."

"How'd they meet?"

"Law school."

"You didn't meet any guys in your college accessorizing classes?" he asked.

"Ha-ha."

"Okay," he said, "so you're looking for a guy with your habits, but what if once you get to know Mr. Perfect, you discover he's not so perfect in bed?"

"Sex is important, but it's not *the* most important part of a relationship."

He chuckled. "I'm pretty sure it is the most important thing."

"If having fun is your only requirement for happiness, then why aren't you with Chantilly or Maisy? All they want is a good time."

Because even the fun girls got tired of their cowboys and it would be only a matter of time before they wandered off the same way as Gunner's mother. "I think we've done enough talking. Ready to sing?"

"I don't sing."

"Then you sit here and enjoy the show." He waved at Zeke. "Time for karaoke." He leaned in and whispered next to Lydia's ear. "Watch and learn, sweetheart. This is how you do fun."

LYDIA'S GAZE FOLLOWED Gunner as he zigzagged through the tables and then stepped onto the dance floor. She couldn't care less that he believed she didn't know the first thing about having a good time—she was just grateful she could finally take a deep breath without his heady scent distracting her.

No man—not even Ryan, her first love and the guy she'd believed was her soul mate—had knocked sensible, determined Lydia off balance the way Gunner did with a simple smile. Except for his good looks, the cowboy was everything she didn't want in a life partner, yet when he spoke, her ears perked and it didn't seem to matter what baloney spewed from his mouth. She attributed her physical reaction to Gunner to the fact that she hadn't been intimate with a man since she'd ended things with Ryan over a year ago. She was young, healthy and…okay, maybe a little horny and that worried her because she couldn't help thinking Gunner might be right and she did need more fun in her life—fun as in a one-night stand with a sexy cowboy.

The door opened and Chantilly and Maisy waltzed into the bar strutting their curvy hips, big hair and flashy rhinestone shirts. They waved at Zeke, their gazes skipping over Lydia.

"The usual?" Zeke called out.

The women nodded, then sat in front of the stage. Zeke delivered two beers to their table.

"Afternoon, folks," Gunner said into the microphone. He winked at the glitter queens. "Ladies."

Chantilly blew a kiss. "Sing me a love song, Gunner."

"'I Swear' by John Michael Montgomery." Maisy ran her tongue over her cherry-painted lips.

Jealousy propelled Lydia off the bar stool and across

the room. She couldn't carry a tune, but that was the least of her cares. Right now she wanted to make sure the buckle bunnies didn't sink their claws into the good-time cowboy, a.k.a. *her* motel manager.

Lydia pasted a smile on her face when Gunner spotted her. "Mind if I join the fun?" She stood in front of him, blocking Maisy's and Chantilly's view.

"You want to sing?" he asked.

"How about a duet?" she said.

"Sure." He held out his hand and helped her onto the stage.

"Think you can handle 'You're the One That I Want' by John Travolta and Olivia Newton-John?"

He shook off her suggestion. "'Jackson' by Johnny Cash and June Carter?"

"Never heard of it."

He chuckled, then spoke into the microphone. "Zeke, pull up the soundtrack from *Grease*, would you?"

A screen lowered from the ceiling. Then music blared from speakers mounted on the walls. Gunner put his arm around Lydia's back and coaxed her closer to the microphone stand. The song lyrics scrolled up the screen and Gunner sang first, his deep voice echoing through the bar.

Holy crap. The cowboy could carry a tune.

And Lydia couldn't. Panic paralyzed her. Then Gunner pressed his fingers into her lower back, the heat from his touch searing the skin beneath her shirt. She sucked in a quick breath, then belted out her verse. Maisy and Chantilly clasped their hands over their ears and grimaced. Even Zeke looked as if he could use a stiff drink. Gunner took over the chorus, drowning her out as she eyed the exit. When her verse came, he twirled her in a circle while she sang, distracting the handful of listeners.

After the song ended, Gunner kissed her. Not a romantic kiss on the lips. Not a hey-that-was-fun-we-should-do-it-again peck on the mouth. But a quick brush against her cheek—the kind of kiss you'd give your eighty-five-year-old aunt. Maisy's and Chantilly's laughter set Lydia's cheeks on fire.

Do it. A voice in her head spoke up.

Why not? Nothing about today had gone as planned.

Lydia grabbed a fistful of Gunner's shirt and pulled him toward her, then rolled up on her tiptoes and pressed her mouth to his. The instant their lips touched, a shiver raced through her body.

One more second… Then she'd stop. But one second turned into two, then three, and then Gunner snuck his tongue between her lips. Whistles and catcalls echoed around them, but the only sound Lydia heard was Gunner's throaty groan and the echo of her answering moan.

Lydia didn't know which one of them finally ended the kiss, but she was pretty sure it wasn't her. She hid her embarrassment behind an exaggerated bow for their audience, then strutted back to her stool.

Gunner sang a country song by Garth Brooks and Maisy and Chantilly danced together, the men cheering them on.

"You got some voice, lady." Zeke refilled her water glass.

"I don't sing very often."

"Sing?" He shook his head. "You sounded like a braying donkey."

She laughed, wishing the tension would leave her body. "Does Gunner perform here often?"

"Every couple of weeks he drops by. He's good for business. The ladies like him."

Another pair of cowgirls walked into the bar and joined Maisy and Chantilly at their table. She studied Gunner's fan club, thinking he could have his pick of females. What type of woman would it take to convince the confirmed bachelor to give up his wild ways? Before she figured out the answer, he left the stage and claimed the stool next to her.

"You're good," she said.

"I know."

"To your ego." She raised her water glass and he tapped his empty beer bottle against the rim.

"To your guts," he said.

"Don't you mean foolishness?"

He shook his head. "You know you have a terrible voice, but you sang anyway. That takes courage."

"Thanks for letting me down easy."

"I'd take bravery in a woman over a pretty singing voice any day."

As far as compliments went, Gunner's had to be at the bottom of her top-ten list. Joking and fun aside, the day was wasting away and she had work to do before her aunt's return to Stampede tomorrow. "I better get going. I need access to the motel rooms to finalize my decorating designs." She held out her hand. "Can I have your office key?"

Gunner pulled out his wallet. "You still plan on using that crazy movie-theme idea?"

Why did he care how the rooms were decorated? She wiggled her fingers under his nose. "Give me the key to the office or you can come back to the motel with me and I'll put you to work."

He tossed a five-dollar bill onto the bar. "I'll follow you."

Surprised, Lydia was momentarily speechless. Once they stepped outside, she found her voice. "Seriously, you should stay here and celebrate your victory." He'd be a huge distraction, especially after they'd kissed. She'd be lucky to keep her mind on her driving, never mind her tasks once they got back to the motel. She hurried to her car, Gunner dogging her heels.

"There's a burger joint down the road. You hungry?"

"Not really."

He reached in front of her and opened the driver-side door. "You sure I can't talk you into stopping somewhere for lunch? My treat."

She shook her head and he laughed as he walked around the hood of his pickup and slid behind the wheel.

They'd driven three miles when Gunner signaled and turned into a gas station. She pulled in behind him, then cursed when he parked at a gas pump. She should have driven on, but like an idiot she waited for him to fill up. Afterward he went into the store, then stepped outside a few minutes later carrying two Slurpees. He walked over to her car and she lowered the window.

"Root beer," he said, handing her the cup.

If she argued that she didn't want a Slurpee, they'd waste even more time. She set the drink in her cup holder. "Thank you."

Gunner returned to his truck and they pulled onto the highway. Twenty minutes later they arrived at the motel and discovered a minivan near room 6. Hector and Maybelle must have left Red in the barn this time. She parked next to Gunner's pickup in front of the office, and as soon as they got out of their vehicles, the motel room door opened and an older couple stepped into view.

Gunner waved and the pair returned the gesture before hopping into the van and driving off.

"Who was that?"

"The Sanderses. They live in Mesquite."

"Don't tell me they have an extra key to the room, also."

"Yep," he said. "The Sanderses had their first—" he waggled his eyebrows "—encounter at the motel and once a month they like to take a stroll down memory lane."

She followed Gunner into the office. He didn't bother turning on the lights. Dark places and Gunner didn't bode well for her, so she flipped on the switch and bright light flooded the room. "How many couples have a key to one of the rooms?"

"Just the Sanderses and Maybelle and Hector." He stepped behind the counter.

"Are you charging the Sanderses for the use of the room?"

"They leave cash on the dresser—whatever they can afford."

"Who changes the bedsheets?" she asked.

"They bring their own. It's part of the deal."

"This is no way to run a business."

"I like to think of it as good customer service."

"I'm surprised none of the rooms have been broken

into and vandalized by delinquents looking for a place to party."

"City kids party in motels, but country boys and girls like to do their drinking and *whatever* in cornfields and haylofts."

"You need to tell the regulars that room 6 is off-limits until after the renovations."

"I don't need to tell them anything. I'm the manager of the place—you're just the decorator."

Lydia hadn't meant to come off sounding condescending. "Look, Gunner. I don't have any hidden agenda. I'm here as a favor to my aunt, whom I love dearly. I want to complete the remodel as quickly as possible and then return to Wisconsin."

"And back to dating cheeseheads."

"My social life is none of your concern."

"You mean love life."

"My love life is fine."

He stepped from behind the counter and stood in front of her, the pearl snaps on his dark blue shirt inches from her nose. "If your love life is fine, then you wouldn't have joined an online dating site."

She opened her mouth, but the rebuttal caught in her throat.

"The right man for you isn't on a dating site."

"How do you know?"

"I know because—" the tender expression in Gunner's eyes rocked her back on her heels "—you're a special lady in a category all by herself."

After all the teasing and mocking, Lydia wasn't sure she believed him.

"And," he said, "if you open yourself up to new experiences, you might discover that what you thought you wanted in a man isn't what you want after all."

"I sang karaoke with you. What other kinds of new experiences are you talking about?"

"Ever had a fling?"

She sucked in a quick breath. "No." Never. Not even close. She'd dated Ryan for almost six months before they'd slept together.

"How many guys have you been with?"

"None of your business." They were supposed to be talking about paint colors and contractors, not sex.

He raised his hand and spread his fingers. "Five?" When she remained silent, he lowered a finger. "Four?" He lowered another finger. "Three?" The peace sign stared her in the face and she nodded.

"You're fibbing," he said. "A beautiful woman like you would have more than a handful of men knocking at her door."

"Sorry to disappoint you. I had my first relationship when I was a sophomore in college and it lasted three years."

"And the second one?"

"A year."

The air sizzled between them. Gunner Hardell wasn't her type—wasn't even close to the guys she'd been paired with on SavvyMatch.com—but there was no denying they were attracted to each other.

His gaze warmed and he tilted his head to the side so the brim of his cowboy hat didn't bump her in the face.

"This isn't a good idea," she said, hoping like crazy that he hadn't heard her.

His lips spread into a grin as he lowered his head. Then his mouth grazed hers before returning a second time to deepen the kiss. When his hands cupped her face and he nuzzled her neck, Lydia knew she was about to have a one-afternoon stand with Gunner Hardell.

Chapter Five

Gunner reached for a room key, his heart pounding harder now than when he climbed onto the back of a rank bronc. He expected Lydia to change her mind, because sex in the middle of the afternoon wasn't her MO, but she just stood there looking at him, face glowing with anticipation.

"Having second thoughts?" she asked.

"I don't want to pressure you." He could deny it all he wanted, but if anyone was feeling under the gun, he was. Lydia rattled him. How was it that a pretty, mature, educated twenty-six-year-old had been with only two men?

Pull yourself together, Gunner.

He took her hand and led her outside and down the sidewalk to room 2, where he then slid the key into the lock.

"I'm having keycard readers installed on the doors," she said.

Gunner made a mental note to keep Lydia's mouth too busy to talk business. He motioned for her to enter the room first, then he followed and hit the light switch. The lamp between the double beds flickered on, casting a warm glow across the beds.

"All the light fixtures will need to be updated." Lydia's gaze traveled around the space, skipping over Gunner.

Was she having second thoughts?

He'd have to bring his A game to keep her focus on him and not the renovations. He flipped the dead bolt, the loud click sealing their fate. He reeled her closer until her breasts bumped his chest. Then he spun her and walked her backward until he had her pinned against the door. He trailed his fingers along her throat, around her neck and up into her hair, where he pulled the pins from her bun.

"The only time I've seen your hair down was at the Valero the first day you arrived in Stampede." He tugged the blond strands until they fell over her shoulders. "It's pretty." And soft. He rubbed his nose against the side of her head. "Smells nice, too." He felt her heart pound hard against his chest. "One request." He lifted his head and stared into her eyes.

She licked her lips. "What's that?"

"We don't talk about the motel." He nuzzled the corner of her mouth. "The only words I want escaping from your sweet lips are 'Oh, Gunner, I love what you do to me.'" He smiled against her throat when she punched his shoulder.

With their mouths firmly locked, he two-stepped her toward the bed, pulled the spread off and then followed her down to the mattress.

There was no turning back now. Hands collided as they fumbled with buttons, zippers and buckles until only bare skin remained between them. He removed a condom from his wallet and placed it on the nightstand, then turned his attention to pleasuring Lydia.

He caressed her body, slow and easy, then fast and hard when her breathing grew shaky. She wiggled a leg between his thighs, wedging herself tighter against him until he didn't know where her body ended and his began. The sting of her nails biting into his back and hips and along his thighs drew a groan from deep inside him.

He pinned her hands to the mattress, then explored her body with his mouth until her squirming threatened to snap his control. He stroked his thumb across her swollen lips and gazed into her eyes. "Are you sure?"

Her tongue snaked out and licked his finger. "Very sure."

There was no turning back now.

THE SOUND OF SNORING woke Lydia from a dead sleep. She opened her eyes and stared at the ceiling. She hated popcorn ceilings. At least the one over her head appeared as if it had never been painted, which would make it easier to scrape off.

"You're hell on a man's ego, Lydia Canter."

The words tickled her belly and she glanced at the dark head resting below her breasts. She didn't dare admit that she'd purposefully tried to focus on anything but the crazy wonderful feeling Gunner's lovemaking had stirred in her.

He lifted himself off her and leaned on his elbow. A sweet warmth spread through her body at the sight of his tussled hair and sleepy grin. He'd been such a considerate lover and she was embarrassed to admit she'd lost track of the number of times she'd whispered, "Do that again, Gunner."

He smoothed his palm over her belly, then cupped her breast. "Did my prowess live up to your expectations?"

She wiggled lower on the bed and kissed him. "You exceeded them."

"So I can safely assume I've taken over first place?"

She laughed. "Your notch on my bedpost is now at the top."

"What's the name of the guy below me?"

"I haven't asked about the women you've slept with." She brushed her mouth over his, then swung her legs off the side of the bed. He caught her wrist.

"Where are you going?"

"I thought we were—"

"Done?" He scowled. "Seriously?" He tugged her back to the mattress and snuggled her against him.

"I need to get some work done today." She traced the brown freckle on the side of his neck.

"Tell me something I don't know about you," he said.

"My favorite number is five."

"Mine's seven."

"What's your favorite color?" she asked.

"Brown."

"Boring brown." Lydia pinched his chest. "Mine's lavender."

"Favorite seafood?" he asked.

"None. Seafood makes me sick. What about you?"

"I love crawfish."

"Yuck."

His fingers tangled in her hair and he closed his eyes. "My mother and I were the only ones in our family who ate crawfish."

"Tell me about your mom."

"I was closest to her. Out of us three boys I resembled her most—at least, that's what Dad always said. She taught me how to catch crawfish with a net and no bait."

"How did she prepare them?"

"We used a propane stove in the backyard. Mom poached them so the meat would soak up the spices in the water."

"When's the last time you ate crawfish?"

"The night before my mother left us." He shifted beneath Lydia as if he tried to escape the memory, but she tightened her arms around him.

"Mom signed me out of school that afternoon and took me crawfish hunting. I didn't think much of it because she was always doing crazy stuff like that."

"Like what?"

"Letting us boys skip school and watch cartoons all day. Eat cereal and ice cream for supper. She let us build a tree house and sleep in it during a thunderstorm." He chuckled. "We got soaked that night from the leaky roof, but it was a blast."

"Your mom sounds like she was a lot of fun."

"She loved to goof off."

Maybe that was why having a good time was important to Gunner—it reminded him of his mother before she'd divorced his father.

Sensing they needed to change the subject, Lydia said, "I need to begin my search for contractors." She made a second attempt to get out of bed, but Gunner tugged her back into his arms and rolled her beneath him.

"I'll let you work as soon as we finish this project." He opened his wallet on the nightstand and removed another condom and set it on the pillow next to Lydia's head. "If I remember right, you liked it when I did this…" He moved his head lower and suddenly Lydia couldn't care less if she got any work done today.

GUNNER TOOK SMALL, shallow breaths, afraid to wake Lydia, who slept curled against his side. Strands of her hair were caught in his whiskers, but he refused to move his head. Instead he tightened his arms around her and imagined what it would be like to wake next to her in bed every morning for the rest of his life— a shocker to say the least. Usually his first thought upon waking tangled up with a woman was how soon he could escape.

After making love with Lydia, he needed to redefine his "type" and come up with a new definition. Not that he was looking to get serious with her—she'd made it clear *he* wasn't her type.

Lydia was looking for Mr. Perfect—a man with a college degree and a 401(k). A guy who put on a suit in the morning and went to the golf course, not a rodeo, on the weekend. A guy who enjoyed sipping fine wine, not singing in karaoke bars. A guy who wanted to get married and a have family, not one who wanted to remain a bachelor.

But he was pretty sure if he *were* all those things Lydia was looking for and not a have-fun-today-and-worry-about-tomorrow-tomorrow kind of guy, then Lydia would consider him her perfect match.

IT WAS DARK inside room 2 the second time Lydia opened her eyes. She held her breath, listening for the sound of Gunner's breathing, but only silence filled her ears.

Any other woman might be heartbroken or miffed to wake up alone in a motel after making love with a man, but not her. She went into the bathroom to rinse off in the shower and found a note on the towel rack. *Got called in to umpire a Little League game.*

For a guy who didn't want kids, he sure jumped at the chance to be around them.

Relieved she'd been spared the awkwardness of facing Gunner after they'd spent hours in bed together, she dressed, then left the room. The sun had dipped low in the sky, reminding her that she'd skipped lunch and dinner.

She got into her car and drove to her aunt's house, then took a proper shower. Dressed in yoga pants and a comfy T-shirt, she perused the contents of the refrigerator. Aunt Amelia ate like a bird—Greek yogurt, applesauce, strawberries and cheese.

Resigning herself to another bowl of cereal, Lydia sat at the kitchen table and checked her email. Her social-worker cousin, Scarlett, asked how long Lydia thought she would be in Stampede. Her other cousin, Sadie, must have forgotten she'd left town, because her email reminded Lydia about Tommy and Tyler's upcoming soccer game. Sadie enrolled the boys in too many supervised activities, but she needed somewhere for them to go after preschool because she worked full-time and her ex always had an excuse for not helping out.

Lydia responded to Sadie, reminding her that she was in Stampede, then sent a message to Scarlett saying she hoped to be back in a couple of weeks. Next she moved on to her work email. A Mrs. Pendergraff wanted to discuss decorating the sunroom in her house. Lydia asked to meet with her at the end of the month—in case it took longer than a few weeks to finish the motel updates.

After she'd taken care of her email, Lydia opened SavvyMatch.com and perused the men who had visited her profile page. She clicked on Mike1211. Not bad looking. Another engineer. Likes golf, enjoys wine-tasting events and is a Bears football fan. Mike lived in Wisconsin, so why wasn't he a Packers fan? *Traitor.* She moved on.

LoverBoy10. He didn't look like much of a lover boy with his thick glasses and receding hairline. She might have been able to get past his appearance, but not the colored socks he wore with khaki shorts and open-toed sandals. *Next.*

JustThe1ForU. *In your dreams, buddy. Next.*

TallManLover. He was too tall. She'd break her neck looking up at him. *Next.*

NiceGuy1978. Too old. *And* none of the men were as good-looking as Gunner.

She logged off the site and opened her designer software program, then studied the plans for the motel rooms, making notes on areas she needed the help of professionals. Afterward, she Googled contractors and wrote down their phone numbers. When she finished, it was eight thirty.

And Gunner still hadn't called or texted her. Was that a good thing or bad thing?

No. No. No. She refused to analyze their tryst at the motel.

She went back to her designs for the rooms and

mulled over which one would get which movie make-over. Twenty minutes later her phone beeped with a text message and Lydia's heart almost pushed through her chest.

Hope you accomplished a lot today. XXOO Aunt Amelia

Lydia's heart dropped back into place. She'd accomplished a lot of *lovemaking*, but that was about it. She texted back.

Looking forward to seeing you tomorrow.

Lydia left the table and made a cup of tea. Whether she went to bed or stayed up, there would be no sleep for her tonight.

Meet me at the motel in twenty minutes.

GUNNER STARED AT the blurry text, then rolled onto his back in room 1. He'd expected Lydia to sleep in this morning after their romp between the sheets late yesterday afternoon, but apparently his studliness hadn't worn her out if she was up and ready to work by 7:00 a.m. on a Sunday morning.

He rolled out of bed and went into the bathroom to take a lukewarm shower. Coffee was next on *his* to-do list. If he wasn't fully awake, he might pound a hole through his hand instead of the wall.

He returned to the office, flipping the sign from Closed to Open. Five minutes later the smell of brewing coffee filled the air and Lydia's blue Civic pulled into the parking lot. The sight of her sent a surge of blood to the part of his body that should have had an out-of-order sign hanging off it. But as soon as the top of her head emerged from the car, he wanted her. *Again*.

His attraction to Lydia confounded him. He would definitely have looked twice at her if they'd bumped into each other on the street, but he still would have kept on walking. Even though she was pretty, her serious demeanor would have raised red flags in his head. He knew it bugged Lydia that he didn't take managing the motel seriously, but the rodeo lifestyle was safe for a guy who wanted only a good time, not forever. However, since he'd already sampled the forbidden fruit, he might as well gorge himself on it as long as he could.

She stepped inside the office and smiled at him. "I'll take a cup of that coffee, please."

It took his brain a moment to process her request. Then he poured a cup of diesel fuel and handed it to her. "I hope you like it strong."

"Perfect." She opened her laptop and tapped the screen, then flipped it toward him. "Here's the game plan for today. I reached out to a few contractors, but there are several things we can do while we wait to hear back from them."

We meaning him.

"I need you to scrape off the popcorn ceiling, tear out the carpet and remove the bathroom countertop in the rooms."

Gunner couldn't believe Lydia was talking *work* after they'd gotten naked with each other yesterday. Hadn't she obsessed over him like he had over her? "Maybe we should wait for the contractor bids to come in."

"It could be a while and we don't have time to waste."

"But it's Sunday."

"And Sunday is demo day." She squeezed his biceps. "I want to see what else these muscles can do besides…" She glanced away, her cheeks turning red.

"Besides holding you close and—"

"Where are your tools?" she asked.

He glanced down at the front of his jeans, then back at Lydia.

"Construction tools." She laughed. "Where do you keep the shovels, paint scrapers and hammers?"

"There's a screwdriver and a wrench in the back room, but that's it." He nodded to the laptop. "Write out a list of stuff you want done and I'll make a trip to one of the home-improvement stores in San Antonio and buy all of the supplies."

"I was hoping to complete the demolition sooner rather than later. I ordered the new carpet for the rooms and it's being delivered in two weeks."

"Whoa." Lydia was moving too fast. If he didn't slow her down, she'd return to Wisconsin before the end of June and his plans for a summer fling would fly right out the window. "I've got a ride in Laredo this Thursday."

She set her coffee down and paced across the room. "Don't you want to do your part to help Stampede get back on its feet again?"

"There's nothing wrong with the town the way it is." Except that it was boring as hell, which was another reason Gunner stuck with rodeo even though he didn't make much money at it—it allowed him to socialize with people his age.

"If more tourists visit," she said, "the motel might become busy enough that you could afford to hire a couple of employees to cover for you when you rodeo."

It was difficult to reconcile the no-nonsense Lydia Canter standing before him with the sexy, naked woman he'd held in his arms just hours ago. "Fixing up one business in this town isn't going to bring all of the tourists back."

"The motel is a good place to start." She pressed her lips together and he sensed she'd argue her case with him all day if he let her.

"I'll help as much as my schedule allows," he said.

"Fine." She took her coffee and sat in the chair in the corner.

"What are you doing?"

"Making the to-do list like you asked for."

"How long before you're finished?" His stomach growled. "I thought I'd grab breakfast at the café."

"You could take off now and get something to eat at a drive-through. Then by the time you reach San Antonio, I'll have texted you the list."

Lydia was definitely back to her old self—all business and no fun.

He nodded to the pot. "Help yourself to another cup."

"Thanks, I will."

Figures he'd get only one cup this morning. He left the office and walked to his pickup. As far as morning-afters went, his and Lydia's was about as exciting as a baked potato.

As soon as Gunner's pickup disappeared down the highway, Lydia allowed herself to relax. She'd been worried that he'd want to discuss their one-night stand and that was the last thing she cared to do. Spending several hours with Gunner in a motel room had been so out of character for her that the only way she could make sense of her behavior was to categorize it as temporary insanity.

She locked the office door and got into her car, then returned to her aunt's house to change clothes. She wasn't going to let the day go to waste. She'd confiscate a few tools from the flower shed in the backyard and begin the demolition work herself. Hopefully the hard labor would take her mind off Gunner.

A half hour later, wearing her black yoga pants and a cotton tank top, Lydia stowed a shovel, rake, hammer, paint scraper and small toolbox in the trunk of her car. When she returned to the motel, she went into the office and got the key to room 5. The logical side of her insisted they start with room 1 and work their way down the line, but she wasn't ready to enter room 2 so soon after she and Gunner had messed up the bed in there. And until Gunner informed the couples who rendezvoused in room 6 that they'd need to search for a different place, she didn't want them dropping by while she was working.

Lydia parked in front of room 5, then propped the door open with a chair. She hadn't been able to bring the ladder in the Civic, but she'd left it on her aunt's front porch and then had texted Gunner asking him to fetch it when he returned to town. First things first— she stripped the linens off the bed, gagging at the yellow stains on the mattress.

By the time she'd dragged the mattress and box spring out of the room by herself, sweat poured off her face and dampened her tank top. A fabric headboard had been bolted to the wall and she used a crowbar to pry it off, taking a huge chunk of plasterboard with it—another repair to add to the to-do list.

She removed the furniture from the room, except for the nightstand, which she used as a stool so she could reach the ceiling. After she tore off a section of bedsheet, she tied the small square of material over her nose and mouth so she wouldn't inhale the dust, then slid on a pair of safety goggles and climbed onto the nightstand.

The table wobbled when she pushed the scraper across the ceiling, but not enough to stop her from working. By the time a horn honked outside the room, she'd scraped half the ceiling clean.

"What the heck do you think you're doing?" Gunner grasped her around the waist and set her on the ground. "You could have fallen and injured yourself."

"I'm not one of your buckle bunnies in constant need of rescuing."

"What did you say?" He tugged off her makeshift mask.

"I said, I'm fine. Did you get the supplies?"

"I did." His gaze skipped around. "It looks like you vandalized the place."

"What took you so long?"

"I ran into a friend I haven't seen in months and we stopped for a beer."

She ignored the urge to ask if the friend was female or male—she didn't want him thinking it mattered to her. "Did you bring the ladder from my aunt's house?"

"Yep." He took her hand and led her outside. "I also brought you lupper."

"What's lupper?"

"The meal between lunch and supper."

On cue her stomach made noise. She followed him into the office, where takeout containers of Chinese food sat on the counter. His thoughtfulness surprised her.

"It'll only take a minute to heat the food," he said. "There's a microwave in the hall storage closet." A minute later Gunner returned to the front desk and offered her a plastic fork. "We'll have to share cooties, because I forgot to ask for plates."

Lydia almost reminded him that they'd shared more than a few cooties in room 2. She sampled the chicken fried rice. "This is good."

"Your aunt called me on the way back to town," he said.

"Really?"

"Amelia tried reaching you, but you didn't answer your phone."

Lydia hadn't heard the ringer over the scraping noise as she'd worked on the ceiling. "What did she want?"

"She's staying in Boerne another day. Said she'd be home tomorrow night."

It was probably best that her aunt didn't know what a dismal start this project had gotten off to. Lydia traded containers with Gunner and sampled the orange chicken. "Thank you for bringing the food."

"Anything to keep the demolition princess happy." The gleam in his eyes said he'd do more than fetch her tools and meals.

She was tempted to let him have his way with her

again, but things could get complicated and she didn't need anything getting in the way of her plans to find Mr. Perfect when she returned to Wisconsin.

Chapter Six

"Done." Gunner descended the ladder, then shook his numb arms until the feeling returned to his fingertips. He glanced around the room. "Lydia?" No answer. He poked his head into the bathroom. Empty. She must have snuck out when he had his back to the door.

He guzzled the bottle of water she'd brought him over an hour ago and admired his handiwork. It was a toss-up as to which job was tougher—riding a bronc or scraping popcorn off a ceiling. Although his arms ached and he had a kink in his neck from tilting his head back for two hours, at least he could cross off the ceilings of rooms 4 and 5 from Lydia's to-do list.

It was after 9:00 p.m. when he stepped outside and spotted her Civic parked by the office. That she was still hanging around the motel this late could mean only one thing—maybe two. She wanted to spend another night with him or she was working on the room designs and lost track of time.

He debated whether to remove the dingy carpet from the rooms or find out why Lydia was still here. His feet made the decision for him and he walked to the office. He understood he wasn't Lydia's type, but the night they'd spent in room 2 proved they were the perfect match in bed. If he wanted to keep her around for the summer, he had to find a way to stall the renovations, which would not please his grandfather.

As if his thoughts had summoned the old man, Emmett's jalopy swung into the lot and Gunner veered off in his direction. Gramps got out of the pickup and hitched his pants.

"Isn't it past your bedtime?" Gunner asked.

"Don't be a smart-ass, boy." He walked over to room 5 and poked his head inside. "That's all you got done?"

"Lydia had me chasing down supplies today."

"Tomorrow haul your backside out of bed before noon."

"What's the big rush? It's not like people are standing in line waiting to reserve a room," Gunner said.

"I'm tired of listening to Amelia bellyache."

"Why do I have a feeling there's more between you and Amelia than a difference of opinion on what to do with this town?"

His grandfather's gaze skipped over Gunner.

"Did you and Amelia butt heads like this in high school?"

Gramps cleared his throat. "No."

"What does that mean?" Gunner asked.

"We got along fine."

"*Fine* as in you had the *hots* for her?" Gunner teased.

"Mind your own business."

"Kind of difficult to do when you hoodwinked me into being Lydia's handyman."

"You got something more important on your calendar?"

The question pricked Gunner's pride. "Rodeo was

good enough when Logan traveled the circuit. How come it's not good enough for me?"

"Your brother made a decent living from busting broncs."

"I'm getting there." The words rang hollow in Gunner's head. "I took first place in Rocky Point yesterday." Not that it meant much, because he didn't live and die rodeo, so he'd never win the big events.

"Gas money," his grandfather grumbled.

"I've got a ride in Laredo on Thursday. Bigger pot."

"Your time would be better spent here."

"The work will get done when it gets done."

Gramps shot him a dark look, then walked outside.

Gunner didn't see what all the fuss was about. If Amelia Rinehart wanted to spend her dead husband's money fixing up an old motel, his grandfather shouldn't care.

Gramps climbed in behind the wheel and Gunner shut the door. "Drive safe." *And stop checking up on me.*

"Was that your grandfather?" Lydia walked toward Gunner.

"He stopped by to check on our progress."

"What did he think?" She stepped toward room 5, but he blocked her and she bumped into his chest.

"You have pretty hair." He brushed a strand from her eyes. "You should wear it down more often." Lydia might act professional, but underneath her all-business-no-play facade, she was every guy's fantasy.

She shifted away from his touch and his arm fell to his side. A tiny wrinkle formed between her eyebrows after she peeked around him into the room. "I thought you'd have removed the carpets tonight."

He hated playing the pity card, but if he didn't do something drastic, she'd bat her eyelashes at him and he'd end up working until midnight. "The carpet has to wait until the kink in my neck goes away. I'm taking a hot shower and then turning in." He left her and went to flip off the lights and lock the doors.

"But it's only nine." She trailed him along the sidewalk. "I was hoping I could talk you into watching a movie with me."

He entered room 1 and she followed him inside, her gaze taking in the clutter. "It looks like someone's been living here."

"Someone does live here."

"Who?"

For a gal with a college degree, she wasn't very perceptive. Maybe a lifetime of eating cheese had clogged the arteries supplying blood to her brain. "This is my room."

"I thought you lived at the ranch with your grandfather and Logan."

"Not all the time." Living under the same roof as his grumpy grandfather and bossy brother had motivated Gunner to find other living arrangements when he was in town between rodeos. "What kind of movie is it?"

"I downloaded *Stagecoach* on my laptop. I need to find a scene from the movie to use as accent wallpaper in room 6."

He tugged off his T-shirt and tossed it onto the chair in the corner. "Viewing an old Western on a laptop screen doesn't sound like much fun."

"But I need a second opinion. And since you're a cowboy…"

He grinned and shrugged out of his jeans.

Her eyes widened. "What are you doing?"

"Taking a shower." His fingers went to the waist-band of his boxers and she twirled her back to him.

"Can't you wait until after the movie?"

He chuckled. "I don't think you want to sit next to me on that bed until I've cleaned up."

"We can watch the movie in the office."

"If you're making me suffer through a boring Western, I'm going to be comfortable and stretch my legs out." He dropped his boxers and went into the bathroom, hoping Lydia would still be around when he finished.

He stepped into the tub and shoved his face beneath the spray. Once he soaped up and rinsed off, he let the water pound against the back of his aching neck. As the muscle pain eased, his thoughts drifted to the day his grandfather had fired Gus, the previous motel manager, and had put Gunner in charge.

"It's a stupid idea, Grandpa." Logan glared at Gunner.

"The boy's got to have an occupation," Gramps said.

Gunner shoved a forkful of beef hash into his mouth. "I've got a profession."

Logan's pointer finger came out. "You're never going to change. You'll always be a goof-off." He spoke to their grandfather. "You can't support Gunner forever. If he needs money, he can feed the cattle, muck the barn or clear debris from the creek."

"Your brother's not a rancher. He can't remember to feed himself, much less a herd of cattle." Gramps rubbed his whiskered jaw. "You've always had a way with charming people."

Gunner kept a straight face. "Mostly the ladies."

"I reckon ladies need motel rooms, too."

"Grandpa!" Logan shoved his fingers through his hair, leaving two tufts sticking up like devil horns. "Don't give him any ideas or he'll turn the motel into a bordello."

"You think you could manage the motel?" Gramps asked.

"How hard can it be?" Gunner asked. "You take a person's credit card number, give them a room key, and that's it."

"What do you do after people check out?" Logan asked.

Gunner shrugged. "Wait for the next person to come along?"

Logan shook his head in disgust.

Gunner loved tormenting his brother—payback for all the times he'd wanted to follow him around after school and Logan had ditched him. If his sibling hadn't been such a pisser all these years, Gunner might have developed a fondness for cattle ranching.

"Gunner doesn't have your dedication, Logan." Gramps stood up and left the room.

"When are you going to grow up and take responsibility for yourself so Grandpa doesn't have to worry about you?" Logan glared from across the room.

"Have I asked any of you to worry about me?"

"Don't make Gramps regret this, you hear?"

Gunner turned off the shower and shook his head, spraying the walls with water. Several years had passed since that "discussion" in the kitchen, but the memory had dogged Gunner's heels every day since, undermining his confidence, making him second-guess himself. And worst of all—Logan had been right. Gunner had been half-assing his job managing the motel, taking advantage of his grandfather's generosity.

And that wasn't even the worst of it.

He was growing bored with rodeo—after a while, falling on his ass wasn't fun. And thanks to meeting Lydia, even the giggling buckle bunnies were losing their appeal.

"Gunner?" Lydia's voice echoed from the other side of the closed door.

"Yeah." He stepped from the tub.

"I ordered pizza to eat while we watch the movie. I figured you'd be hungry."

Stampede didn't have a pizza business. She must have called someplace in Rocky Point. He knotted a towel around his waist and opened the door. "What kind of pizza?"

"Pepperoni and extra cheese."

He padded across the floor, then stopped in front of her and tipped her chin up until she looked him in the eye. "How did you know pepperoni and cheese is my favorite?"

"I didn't. I ordered my favorite."

"How long before they deliver it?"

"An hour and a half." Her gaze softened.

Gunner knew what she was thinking—the same as he was. He swooped her into his arms and carried her to the bed…

Two and a half hours later with their bellies full of pizza, Lydia hit the pause button on her laptop, which rested on Gunner's naked chest. "What do you think of this image?"

Gunner cracked an eye open. "It looks the same

as the last one. Horses, mesquite, rocky ground and a blazing sun."

"Really?" She moved the laptop up his chest, closer to her face. "But the clouds are different."

"A cloud is a cloud." He caressed Lydia's back, more than a little surprised at how right she felt in his bed. In his arms.

"We definitely need to pick a scene with John Wayne riding a horse." She hit the pause button a second time and the movie continued playing. "This one might work."

Gunner closed his eyes and breathed in Lydia's sweet scent. "Have you ever ridden a horse?" he asked her.

"No."

"You visited your aunt in Texas when you were younger. Didn't your parents take you on a trail ride?"

"My parents aren't the outdoorsy type."

Lydia would look cute in a pair of Wranglers and cowgirl boots. "I could teach you how to ride. We've got a couple of old nags out at the ranch."

She closed the computer and set it aside, then rolled on top of Gunner. "The only stud I'm interested in riding is you."

LYDIA WAS ALONE in bed Monday morning when she woke up in Gunner's room. She stretched against the cool sheets, smiling at the memory of eating pizza and watching a movie in bed with him. When her gaze shifted to the popcorn ceiling, her smile vanished.

She couldn't keep sleeping with Gunner—she didn't want their relationship to get in the way of the work that needed to be done at the motel. Then again, she'd love to meet the woman strong enough to turn Gunner down when he wore nothing but a skimpy towel, his bare chest glistening with water drops.

Maybe she was making things more difficult than she needed to. She was a big girl. If she wanted a hot fling with a sexy cowboy while she was in town, then why not? It wasn't like anything would come of their affair. And just to prove she could remain emotionally detached from Gunner, she turned on the lamp and opened her laptop to check her dating profile. It was only a matter of time before one of the men hit all the marks with her.

She clicked on Jacob4Life. Age thirty-two. Not bad looking. His jaw wasn't as chiseled as Gunner's, but he had kind eyes. He enjoyed cycling, not rodeo—that was a plus. He was wearing a dress shirt in his photo, not a tight T-shirt like Gunner wore. Jacob's hair was neatly combed and trimmed, not shaggy like Gunner's. He worked in management for a telecommunications company and enjoyed taking his nephews to baseball games. He must like children and want kids of his own—unlike Gunner. Before she lost her nerve, she pinged Jacob back.

On to WorldTraveler5. Age thirty-four. He'd left his height blank, which meant he wasn't tall. Gunner wasn't a giant, but in his boots he stood at least six feet. Lydia had no idea how long she'd been studying dating profiles when the door flew open and Gunner waltzed in carrying a box of pastries and two hot coffees. "'Morning, princess."

She closed the laptop and returned his smile, hoping her warm cheeks didn't make her look guilty. "How thoughtful of you to bring food."

He set their breakfast on the nightstand, then removed his shirt.

She gaped. "What are you doing?"

"If we're eating in bed and you're not wearing any clothes, then I shouldn't, either." He dropped his jeans to the floor but thankfully kept his boxers on and then slid beneath the covers next to her.

"You're such a goof-off," she said, his charming behavior winning her over. She had a feeling if she stayed in bed with Gunner, he'd change her mind about a whole lot of things, including the cowboy himself. She handed him a coffee and a doughnut. "I didn't know Stampede had a bakery."

"They don't. I bought these at the Valero down the road."

Thoughtful and considerate—qualities she was looking for in an online match. He bit into a doughnut and jelly squirted out the side, plopping onto his bare chest.

She scraped the glob off, then stuck her finger into her mouth. "Raspberry."

"I thought they were cherry filled." He brushed his mouth against hers and then snuck his tongue inside. "Raspberry. You're right." He settled against the headboard, then reached for her laptop. "Which spaghetti Western are you watching now?" When he saw the dating site pop up, he said, "I guess my technique needs some work."

She cringed. Fling or not, no guy wanted his lover perusing a dating site the morning after.

"He's too old for you," Gunner said.

"Who?"

"WorldTraveler5."

"He's only eight years older." She bit into her dough-nut. "Besides, I'm ready to have a child right after I get married."

"If you want a baby that bad, go to a sperm bank."

"No, thanks. I want to have a baby the traditional way—with a husband."

He nodded to the laptop. "Older guys are soft around the middle."

Lydia licked the sugar off her lips as she studied Gunner's naked chest. "There are plenty of attractive older men." She wasn't sure if she was trying to convince him or her.

"Older guys are boring and set in their ways."

She nudged him with her elbow. "How do you know? Have you dated one?"

Laughter rumbled in his chest. "The dairy princess has a wicked sense of humor."

She blamed Gunner for bringing out the sass in her.

He reached across her and set his coffee on the nightstand, then did the same with hers. Next he closed the pastry box and leaned over to place it on the other bed. When he straightened, he stared into her eyes.

Any woman who claimed she didn't enjoy a man devouring her as if she were a piece of food was touched in the head. "Gunner."

His breath puffed against her face. "What, princess?"

"We have work to do."

"Why the rush? The motel isn't going anywhere."

"I can't stay all summer." *I want to, but...* "I have to get back to Wisconsin and focus on my business."

His attention shifted to the laptop next to her thigh and she assumed he thought she was eager to start dating. She held her breath—half hoping he'd storm out the door and half wishing he'd kiss her and make her forget her dating profile.

He kissed her. Thank goodness.

"WHAT ARE YOU doing here?" Logan asked when he walked into the ranch house and found Gunner sitting at the kitchen table in the middle of the day. "Don't you have some rodeo to ride in?"

To be honest, Gunner couldn't think about rodeo or much else since he'd begun sleeping with Lydia. "Have you heard from Reid lately?"

"No. Why?"

Gunner was stalling. "I thought since Gramps isn't helping out as much around the ranch..."

"You came here to tell me that you don't think I can handle the ranch?"

Dang, his brother was touchy. "No." Gunner decided not to beat around the bush. "I need some advice."

Logan grabbed a bottle of water from the fridge. "Advice on finding a real job?"

"Very funny." Gunner slid his chair back. He should have known his sibling would hassle him.

"Stay right where you are." Logan sat down at the table. "You drove all the way out here, so spill your guts."

Now that he had his brother's ear, Gunner wasn't sure what kind of guidance he was asking for. Maybe he was just looking for someone to set him straight about Lydia. "I met a girl...a woman I really like."

"Lydia Canter."

"How did you know?"

"I ran into Hector at the hardware store in Mesquite. He said you're sharing your motel room with her."

"Does everyone know?"

"Maybelle has a big mouth."

Gunner groaned. "What about Gramps?"

"If he does, he hasn't said anything to me."

If their grandfather found out he was wasting time with Lydia instead of working on the renovations, the geezer would threaten to remove him as the manager. Gunner liked his current living arrangement and didn't want to bunk at the ranch and put up with his brother's bad moods.

"What kind of advice do you want?" Logan asked.

"When you met Beth, was she seeing other guys?"

Logan dropped his gaze and Gunner regretted bringing up his brother's ex-wife, but he had to get his head on straight where Lydia was concerned.

"Neither of us was dating anyone else when we met. Why?"

"Lydia's using one of those online dating sites."

"Dating around is one thing—sleeping around is another."

Exactly. Lydia wasn't sleeping with any of her supposed perfect matches—yet. So why did it bother Gunner that she was considering contacting WorldTraveler5?

"I get it now," Logan said.

"What?"

"You're jealous of the guys on the dating site." Logan chuckled. "This must be a first for you." He snapped his fingers. "Or…"

"What?"

"You're upset because Lydia isn't into you as much as you're into her."

"She's into me." If she wasn't, then she put on a

good act in bed. "She's on the dating site because she's ready to settle down."

"And you aren't. So it shouldn't matter to you that she's looking at potential husbands as long as it's not you, right?"

A couple of weeks ago Gunner would have agreed with his brother.

"Look," Logan said, "you've always insisted you don't want to get married, and to be honest, that's probably pretty smart of you, since you suck at being a rodeo cowboy and a motel manager."

"Once the motel is fixed up, I'll have to stick around more if tourists return to Stampede."

Logan shook his head. "Fresh paint and new bedspreads aren't going to bring people back to town when there's nothing for them to do once they get here."

"If the motel doesn't stay busy, then I'll go back to busting broncs."

"Didn't you hear the part where I said you suck at rodeo?"

"I'll work harder at it."

"You're twenty-seven. If you haven't won a buckle yet, chances are you won't."

"So I'm supposed to quit rodeo like you quit on your marriage?" Gunner held his breath when Logan's face turned crimson. His brother hadn't contested his divorce when Beth served him papers. Hadn't even insisted on marriage counseling.

"You can try all you want, Gunner, but you'll eventually learn you can't outrun who you are."

"What the hell is that supposed to mean?"

"You're too laid-back to ever put 110 percent into

anything you do. Some people are just meant to coast through life and you're one of them."

This wasn't the helpful advice he'd hoped to receive from his brother. "Thanks a lot for the pep talk."

"Gunner?"

He paused at the back door. "What?"

"It isn't always the hardworking guys—" meaning Logan "—who finish last. Sometimes the charmers do, too."

Chapter Seven

C'mon, pick up. Lydia sat in the Cattle Drive Café Thursday morning, waiting to meet Aunt Amelia for breakfast. Her call went to Gunner's voice mail—for the third time in thirty minutes. When his sexy voice invited her to leave her name and number, she hung up.

"You're frowning." Her aunt tossed her purse onto the seat across from Lydia, then slid into the booth. "What's the matter?"

"We're halfway through the first week in June and Gunner's AWOL and the contractors I reached out to aren't returning my messages."

Dolly headed toward their table with a coffeepot and glasses of water, saving Lydia from confessing that little progress had been made on the renovations since Gunner had scraped the ceilings in rooms 4 and 5 and torn out the carpet.

"You're looking lovely as ever, Amelia." Dolly filled the white mug, then topped off Lydia's cup. "Yellow is definitely your color."

"Thank you, Dolly. What's Bud working on now?"

"A TV stand for a young couple in Mesquite."

"He should open a shop in Stampede." Amelia nodded to Lydia. "Bud's a talented woodworker. He made the hutch in my dining room."

"If you succeed in bringing tourists back to this town, he might consider renting space in one of the vacant stores."

"Once the Moonlight Motel is renovated, I have another idea I'm working on to entice people to visit Stampede," Amelia said.

"Emmett's been telling everyone who'll listen that the rest of the town is off-limits to you."

Amelia winked. "We'll see about that."

"You should run for mayor the next election. Emmett's held the office for too long," Dolly said.

"Don't worry about Emmett. He'll see the light eventually."

"I hope you're right. The café is barely breaking even." Dolly tugged a pencil from behind her ear and flipped open her order pad. "The usual?"

Amelia nodded, then Dolly looked at Lydia. "You having oatmeal and a banana, too?"

"That sounds fine."

After Dolly left, Lydia opened her prescription bottle.

"You're still taking medicine for your sinus infection?"

After swallowing the pill, she said, "That was the last one."

"Are you getting enough rest, dear? You look tired."

Tossing and turning in bed thinking about Gunner had robbed her of sleep the past couple of nights. If her aunt had heard through the grapevine that Lydia had spent time in Gunner's motel room, she didn't mention it. "The remodel is taking longer than necessary because Gunner isn't the most reliable worker."

And when he is in town, he's preoccupied. With me.

"You haven't had any luck with contractors?"

Lydia shook her head. "I can't find a work crew willing to make the drive out here." She sipped her water. "If we're stuck with Gunner's help, fixing up the motel will take the entire summer." And Lydia couldn't stay that long—not only because her design business would suffer, but because if she and Gunner slept together more than a handful of times, it would no longer be a fling but a relationship. And she wanted her next relationship to be with a potential perfect match from the dating site.

"Here you go, ladies." Dolly set their food on the table. "Anything else I can get for you?"

"No, thank you. This looks wonderful," Amelia said.

"Holler if you need refills on the coffee."

After Dolly walked off, Lydia said, "The people here are so friendly. It's not always like that in a large city."

"Don't let this small town fool you. We have a few unfriendlies here, too."

"You mean Gunner's grandfather?"

"Emmett wasn't always cantankerous."

"I don't mean to pry..." Lydia smiled. "Yes, I do." Her aunt laughed. "Why do I get the sense that there's more between you and the mayor than butting heads over Stampede?"

"There has always been more between us—we've just never discussed it." Her aunt's gaze shifted to the windows.

"Did you and Emmett do more than date when you were in high school?"

"Heavens, no."

Lydia grasped her aunt's hand. "Do you regret that?"

Amelia's smile shook around the edges. "Maybe a

little." She shrugged. "Sara was a better match for Emmett's temperament."

"Was Emmett happily married to her?"

Amelia pushed the oatmeal around in her bowl. "It took him a little time, but eventually he realized Sara was a great catch."

"And you were happy with Uncle Robert?"

"We were well suited for each other."

Lydia ate her oatmeal in silence. Suited didn't sound very romantic. Was that what she was searching for in a husband—a man who *suited* her? She shoved the thought away and said, "If we don't find a contractor, I don't see how we'll get the renovations done anytime soon."

Her aunt pulled out her cell phone and made a call. "Sylvie, does your nephew still do plumbing on the side? I see. Okay, thank you."

Lydia sat quietly, eating her banana while Amelia made phone calls. Fifteen minutes and more than a few conversations later, her aunt set the phone aside.

"No luck?" Lydia asked.

Amelia shook her head. "Finish your breakfast. Then we'll take a drive out to Paradise Ranch and pay Emmett a visit."

Amelia left twenty dollars on the table, then put her banana in her purse and took a sip of coffee before vacating the booth and marching out the door. Lydia drove them to the ranch in the Civic and parked behind Emmett's rust-bucket pickup sitting in front of the rambling wood-and-stone one-story.

"Every time I see this house, I become angry." Amelia released her seat belt. "Sara had this front yard looking so beautiful before she got sick." Amelia pointed out the windshield. "The crepe myrtle trees barely bloom anymore because the boys haven't cut them back in years. That area over there—" Amelia's finger swung in the opposite direction "—the knockout rose bushes barely bloom because they've been neglected so badly. And who knows what they did with the porch swing that Sara loved sitting on at the end of the day. This used to be a home that welcomed people. Sara would be hurt if she knew how badly Emmett and her grandsons have neglected it."

"I don't have a green thumb, but Sadie does. She's in charge of selecting the plants and flowers for her apartment complex and works with the association on the gardens."

"I need to take a trip north, don't I? It's been a couple of years since I last saw Tommy and Tyler."

"The boys run circles around Sadie." Lydia followed her aunt, but they both stopped at the porch steps when the front door opened and Emmett walked outside.

"Little early for a social call," he said.

"Don't give me that." Amelia climbed the steps. "You haven't slept past dawn since you got married."

"How would you know?"

"Sara told me."

"What else did Sara say about me?"

"Plenty." Amelia paused on the top step. "Invite us in for coffee."

"If I don't?"

"I'm not leaving until you hear me out, stubborn old man."

Emmett's eyes gleamed as if he looked forward to bickering with Amelia. "Guess I better put a pot of coffee on, then." He returned inside, leaving the door open.

Lydia and her aunt walked down a narrow hallway toward the back of the house, Lydia peeking inside each room they passed by. The wood moldings and large windows were beautiful, but the mismatched furniture, outdated drapes and clutter in every room begged for a woman's touch.

Aunt Amelia sat at the oak table in the middle of the kitchen and Lydia joined her. The room looked as tired as the rest of the house—gray Formica countertops, black appliances covered in fingerprints and linoleum floor with black scuff marks from a decade's worth of cowboy boots stomping across it. The one bright spot in the room was the red ceramic rooster sitting on the counter next to the coffeemaker.

Emmett flipped the switch on the machine, then removed three mugs from the cupboard before leaning against the counter and crossing his arms over his chest. "I'm listening."

"We're having trouble finding contractors willing to drive this far to do a job."

"I've called everyone within an hour's drive of Stampede," Lydia said, "but none of them are returning my calls."

"Isn't Gunner helping?" Emmett glanced between Lydia and her aunt.

"Yes, Gunner's helping, but I need electrical and plumbing contractors. We have to make sure the work is up to code."

The timer on the coffeemaker dinged. Emmett poured the brew, then set the mugs on the table and took a seat. "What do you want me to do? Round up a bunch of contractors at gunpoint?"

"I want you to use your charismatic personality and find someone who will help us," Amelia said.

Emmett's gaze slid over Amelia and there was no mistaking the appreciation in his eyes. Lydia bet Gunner's grandfather had a crush on her aunt.

"Apparently our local contractors, Mr. Peterson, Mr. Kimble and Mr. Andrew, aren't available to help with the renovations because they're busy with other projects." Amelia tapped a fingernail on the table. "I don't know of anyone else around here who has experience in construction."

Emmett squinted as he blew on his hot coffee. "You ever consider no one's available to help because they're trying to avoid you?"

"What's that supposed to mean?" Amelia asked.

"Only that you stick your nose into everyone's business."

"I'm trying to help this town, which is more than you've done since becoming mayor."

"Stampede doesn't need help. It's fine the way it is."

"I'm not going to get into that argument with you again, Emmett. I came out here to ask for your help."

"You have help. You should be thanking me for letting your niece have Gunner."

The sip of coffee in Lydia's mouth took a detour down her throat and ended up in her lungs, sending her into a coughing fit. Emmett and Amelia ignored her.

"Gunner means well, but he doesn't have the dedication to see this project through," Amelia said.

Emmett's gaze swung to Lydia. "Never heard a woman yet complain about his dedication."

Lydia ignored the innuendo and said, "I tried reaching Gunner today, but he's not answering his phone."

"Think he went to a rodeo in Laredo," Emmett said.

Amelia slapped her palm on the table and Lydia jumped. "If we can't count on Gunner's help, then it's your responsibility to hire someone else."

He set his mug down with way too much care. "Don't forget who owns that motel."

"And if you want to keep it, then you'll cooperate," Amelia said.

The air in the room evaporated when the older couple locked gazes.

Amelia rose from her chair. "If I were you, I'd advise Gunner to put his rodeo career on hold until you find a contractor to replace him." She slid her mug toward Emmett. "And for goodness' sake, learn how to make a decent cup of coffee."

"Got too much kick-ass for you, Amelia?"

"There's only one person in this room that needs an ass-kicking."

Lydia held her breath, afraid Emmett would unleash his furor at her aunt, but instead he chuckled at Amelia's retreating back.

"LADIES AND GENTLEMEN, next up on this sweltering Saturday afternoon is the saddle-bronc competition. Gunner Hardell from Stampede, Texas, is the first cowboy out of the chute."

The mediocre round of applause echoing through the stands of the fairgrounds might have depressed Gunner if not for the feminine catcalls from the buckle bunnies camped next to the chutes. He could always count on the lovelies to feed his ego.

He climbed the rails, then tipped his hat to the handful of onlookers. The ladies whistled, and when his eyes landed on a blonde in the group, for a split second he thought Lydia had come to watch him. The woman was pretty—most of them were. But her mouth didn't turn up at the corners when she smiled like Lydia's did. Her face was more round than oval and her chin didn't have that stubborn tilt to it like Lydia's.

He slid a leg over Reckless and settled on the bronc's back. Not a muscle in the horse twitched and Gunner's adrenaline kicked up a notch. He preferred a fidgety bronc in the chute—a foe he could count on to bust out on all four cylinders. The quiet ones were too hard to read and he didn't like surprises when the gate opened.

Lydia's face flashed before his eyes. He hadn't returned any of her calls since sneaking out of town on Thursday. He couldn't very well tell her that he was purposefully putting the brakes on the renovation to try to keep her in Stampede.

Stop thinking about Lydia and pay attention to what you're doing or this beast will stomp your head.

"Heard Reckless likes to spin before he bucks." Ernie Jones balanced himself on the rails next to Gunner.

Gunner's and Ernie's careers mirrored each other—they'd begun rodeoing around the same time and neither of them had been very successful.

"What's the matter?" Ernie asked.

"Nothing. Why?"

He nodded at Gunner's gloved hand, which rested on the rail. "You gonna grab the rope or ride with both hands in the air?"

Jeez. Gunner wound the rope around his gloved hand. If he didn't find a way to shut Lydia out of his thoughts, he might as well not even leave the chute.

"Good luck, man." Ernie dropped to the ground.

Gunner closed his eyes and focused on his breathing. *In. Out. In. Out.* He opened his eyes and gave a curt nod to the gateman. Everything went downhill from there.

Reckless sprang from the chute and spun right, the action twisting Gunner's spine and throwing his hips off balance. He could blame the horse's inherent nastiness for catching him unawares, but it was the memory of Lydia's soft smile as she lay beneath him when he…

Gunner went flying off the back of the bronc— him in one direction, his hat in the other. The feeling of weightlessness lasted only a second before the hard dirt knocked the air from his chest. Instinct kicked in and he rolled away from the vibrations in the ground— putting as much distance between him and the pounding hooves as he could. The rodeo helpers caught the horse's rein and the animal trotted like royalty out of the arena.

Gunner crawled to his feet and swiped his hat off the ground. His shoulder was numb, but he managed to wave at the crowd as he strolled back to the cowboy ready area, where Ernie waited. "What the hell happened, man? You lasted two seconds before Reckless kicked your ass."

"Got distracted." Gunner removed his spurs and tossed them into his gear bag. A rodeo worker returned his saddle and rope. "Thanks, man."

Ernie kept talking, but Gunner didn't hear a word. His thoughts had drifted to Lydia—again. He'd missed her the past two days. She wasn't as flashy as the buckle bunnies he usually dated but just as sexy—maybe even more so because she didn't flaunt her finer attributes. When a man looked at Lydia, he had to really look—

study her to see her sexy curves, the slope of her neck… the gentle swell of her buttocks. Like a soft feather bed, Lydia had the kind of body a man could sink into and never find his way out of.

"Earth to Gunner," Ernie said.

He shook his head. "What were you saying?"

"You gotta keep your head on straight or the next time you'll get hurt. Reckless came this close—" the cowboy pinched his fingers together "—to stomping your skull."

Ernie was right. If Gunner couldn't keep his head in the game, then he shouldn't be riding. And as long as Lydia was in Stampede working on the motel, he didn't stand a chance of succeeding at rodeo. "I guess I need to take a break."

"What do you mean?"

"A vacation from rodeo."

"Since when has rodeoing ever been work?"

"Since I got something better waiting for me in Stampede."

"When you coming back?"

"End of the summer." When Lydia returned to Wisconsin.

"You lucky son of a gun." Ernie glanced at the buckle bunnies. "Which one?"

"She's not one of them." What did it matter if he told his buddy about Lydia? It wasn't like he'd run into her. "Her name's Lydia and she's renovating the motel in Stampede."

"I thought you liked the motel just the way it is—a dump."

"I did…still do, but this is my grandfather's doing."

Ernie grinned. "You don't like the renovations, but you like the renovator."

"It's nothing serious."

"Nothing with you is ever serious. Maybe I'll stop by and check out your new digs."

"You do and I'll punch your face."

Ernie's laughter echoed through Gunner's brain long after the cowboy walked off. He'd snuck out of Stampede early Thursday morning after he'd woken in a cold sweat from a dream where he'd been looking at engagement rings in a jewelry store.

Marriage wasn't in his plans—especially to a woman like Lydia. She was too serious. Too...together. It was okay to *like* her, admire her talents and her generosity toward her great-aunt. But anything more would lead him down the path to a broken heart. He might not be the brightest bulb in the chandelier, but he was smart enough to know a woman like Lydia would never pick a guy like him to be her forever man.

The only thing Gunner was certain about right now was that if he didn't want a broken neck, rodeo would have to wait until Lydia left Stampede.

Chapter Eight

Lydia turned off the wallpaper steamer in room 3 and checked the time on her phone. "It's five thirty." She smiled at Karl, the contractor Emmett had found to help her with the motel renovations. "You were supposed to quit at five."

"I wanted to finish tearing out the carpet in room 6. Is there anything else you need me to do before I take off?"

"Nope. You were a huge help today."

He shifted from one work boot to the other, his gaze skipping over Lydia. "I appreciate you letting me bring the girls along."

Karl Schmidt lived in Mesquite and was a divorced father of two daughters, ages seven and nine, and Lydia guessed he was around thirty-five years old. He was average looking but had kind eyes and worked his tail off—unlike a certain cowboy who'd rather rodeo than help her. "Nicole and Gaby are sweet girls. I feel bad that you worked during your weekend with them."

"They did the same thing here that they do at my house."

The sisters had played school in the motel office after Lydia's aunt had dropped off coloring books and craft supplies earlier in the day.

Karl offered a shy smile. He seemed like a good father who might not be opposed to having more children, but a man like him was Lydia's backup plan. She really wanted to find a guy who hadn't ever been married and preferably had no children. If that didn't happen by the time she was thirty, then she'd consider becoming part of a blended family.

"The girls' mother is picking them up at seven." Karl organized his toolbox.

"What are you doing here, Schmidt?"

"Hey, Gunner." Karl offered his hand. "Your grandfather asked me to pitch in and help with the remodeling."

Gunner walked farther into the room, his eyes shifting between Karl and Lydia. "I thought I heard you'd moved to Mesquite after your divorce."

"I did." Karl edged toward the door. "Stacy settled there after she remarried and it's easier to share custody of our daughters if we live in the same town." He looked at Lydia. "I better get the girls."

"I'll go with you and say goodbye to them." Lydia followed Karl, her shoulder brushing against Gunner's chest when he didn't give her room to pass by him. She caught a hint of his familiar aftershave and breathed deeply through her nose. He always smelled so good. She expected him to follow, but he remained behind in the room.

She gave the girls a hug and thanked them for being good, then waved until Karl's truck disappeared down the highway. When she turned back to the motel, she spotted Gunner wielding the wallpaper steamer through the open door. She hurried across the parking lot, worried he'd ruin her progress. "I'll take over," she said when she entered room 3.

"I've got it." He stepped sideways, blocking her when she made a grab for the machine.

"Aren't you tired after a long day rodeoing?"

"Eight seconds is hardly a long day."

"So you didn't get bucked off in Laredo?" she asked.

He flashed his white-toothed grin. "As a matter of fact, I did." He set the steam wand aside and peeled off a sheet of brown, orange and gold-flecked wallpaper. "That was my last rodeo for the summer."

"Why?"

"I'm committed to helping you with the motel."

Now that she had a professional contractor, the last thing Lydia *needed* was Gunner hanging around getting in the way. "That's not necessary. You go ahead and rodeo. Karl and I have things under control here."

"Three hands are better than two, right?"

She hadn't meant to make it sound as if she preferred Karl's help to Gunner's—even if she did. Besides, it hadn't been very nice of him to take off without telling her when he'd be back. They weren't in a relationship, but they'd slept together and she deserved a little consideration.

He turned off the steamer and headed for the door. "I'll remove the carpet in the rest of the rooms."

"Karl took care of it. But you could arrange to have the Dumpster emptied again."

"Okay, sure."

A half hour later, Lydia finished removing all of the wallpaper in the room and was just about to go in search of Gunner when he appeared in the doorway.

"They're coming tomorrow to empty the Dumpster. What else can I do?"

"Remove the carpet in room 1." She hadn't let Karl into Gunner's private quarters.

"My room is off-limits," he said. "I noticed the popcorn has been removed from all the ceilings."

"Except yours."

Gunner ignored her and said, "Should I start on the bathroom tile tomorrow?"

"I changed my mind about new tile for the bathrooms. I think it will be fine if Karl replaces the cracked ones in each bathroom and then we'll clean the grout really well."

"So there's nothing left for me to do?"

The teasing glint Lydia was accustomed to seeing in Gunner's eyes fizzled out. "I thought you'd be happy that we hired Karl," she said. "The sooner I'm finished, the sooner I'm out of your way." *And out of your bed.*

He shoved his fingers through his hair. "I don't care if you hired Karl."

Then why was he so agitated? "Did something happen at the rodeo?"

"No."

The one-syllable answer sounded like a cussword as he reached behind him and closed the door. The snick of the dead bolt echoed in her ears. Gunner moved toward her, tugging at the snaps of his Western shirt, then letting it drop to the floor behind him.

She picked up the steamer wand and pointed it at his muscled chest. "Don't take another step."

He stopped in front of her, the wand pushing into his chest when he lowered his mouth toward hers. "Kiss me, Lydia."

She dropped the wand to the floor and wound her arms around his neck, then did exactly as he asked.

GUNNER'S NOT YOUR TYPE.

How many times had Lydia told herself that, then as soon as he so much as looked sideways at her, she fell into his arms.

She pressed her hand to her stomach as a sudden wave of nausea hit her. Great. She'd finally kicked the ear infection only to come down with the flu. Or maybe it was a slight case of food poisoning after eating the chicken enchiladas Gunner had fetched for them last night from the Cattle Drive Café.

A full week had passed since he'd promised to quit rodeo until the motel update was completed. She appreciated his offer to help, but now that Karl was working on the project, Gunner was at loose ends. Lydia did her best to run interference between the two men and assign Gunner tasks that wouldn't interfere with Karl's work, but Gunner still managed to get in the contractor's way.

"What's the matter, dear?" Aunt Amelia carried the mail into the kitchen Saturday afternoon. "You look befuddled."

She was confused—mostly about her feelings for Gunner. None of the men on the dating site who'd been matched with her had the cowboy's good looks or sexy grin. "I can't decide if we should use a neutral color in the rooms or go with custom paint shades," Lydia said.

Amelia sat at the table. "If you're worried about money, don't be."

"It's not the money," Lydia said. "I keep thinking a

bold color would detract from the movie-scene wall-paper in the room."

"You're probably right. What are the choices for neutral colors?"

Lydia clicked on the paint samples and several colors popped up on the laptop screen. "How about that one?" Amelia tapped her nail against a sample with pink undertones.

"The decorations and bed linens will be on the cooler side, so we need to keep the paint undertones in the purple, blue and green category." Lydia pointed to the third row of swatches. "Do you like any of these?"

"That one looks nice." Amelia indicated the white with blue undertones.

"I like it, too." Lydia made a note in the file to order Decorator White from the home-improvement store. When she finished, she found her aunt studying her. "Don't tell me you changed your mind already?"

Amelia's eyes narrowed. "I'm a member of the Stampede Women's League."

It took Lydia a moment to switch her train of thought.

"Ruby called this morning. She saw you and Gunner kissing yesterday when she drove past the motel."

Lydia ducked her head, willing her cheeks not to turn red. What rotten timing. Ruby must have caught the thank-you kiss she'd given Gunner when she'd opened the room door and found him holding their supper.

She forced herself to meet her aunt's gaze. "Gunner and I… It's… He's…" Lydia's forehead broke out in a sweat.

"I may be old, dear, but I remember what it was like

to be young and swept away by passion." Amelia's expression softened, the wrinkles around her mouth relaxing. "Gunner's a handsome man and you're a very pretty woman. Of course you two would be attracted to each other."

"You're not upset?"

"Should I be?"

"You don't like Gunner's grandfather."

"I like Emmett just fine when he stays out of my way." She winked. "There's nothing wrong in enjoying yourself while you're in town."

Lydia sensed a *but* coming.

"As long as you're careful. Gunner's a sweet-talker, but he's irresponsible and I doubt the young man will ever settle down."

"I know. Men like Gunner can't be counted on for anything but a good time."

Amelia frowned. "You've looked pale the past few mornings."

She had?

As if on cue, Lydia's stomach lurched into her throat and she sprang from the chair. Luckily, her aunt's home had a half bath in the hallway outside the kitchen. She stumbled into the tiny room and offered up her stomach contents to the porcelain god.

After retching for the third time, Lydia flushed the toilet, then sat on the lid and waited for her head to stop spinning.

"Here." Aunt Amelia held out a damp washcloth.

Lydia pressed it against her eyes. "I think I have food poisoning."

"Is it coming out the other end, too?"

"Not yet." Lydia laughed. "Don't worry—I'll be fine."

"I don't think it's food poisoning."

"What else could it be?"

Her aunt's gray eyebrows drew together. "There's no chance you're pregnant?"

"We used protection." Every single time.

"You or Gunner used protection?"

"Gunner."

"Condoms aren't foolproof, dear."

Aunt Amelia's sympathetic smile made Lydia's eyes water and the tears she'd tried holding at bay spilled down her cheeks. "You don't think it's food poisoning?"

"Do you?"

She wished with all her heart it was, but her gut insisted otherwise. Lydia's lip wobbled. "No." Why did this have to happen with Gunner? Why couldn't it have been with a man who was mature, ready to settle down and wanting a family?

Her aunt stroked Lydia's hair. "It's going to be okay."

How? She was pregnant. Single. And no man in his right mind would choose to date a pregnant woman. She wrapped her arms around her aunt and blubbered. "I was finally ready to start looking for Mr. Right."

"A baby won't stop you from finding a man to build a life with."

Yeah, right. All she had to do was look at Sadie, her divorced cousin and a mother of two boys, to know most men ran the opposite way when they found out a woman had kids. After Sadie told her dates she was a mom to twins, they never asked her out again.

"There's no need to get worked up until you know

for sure. Your ear infection or the stress of the motel renovations might have caused your cycle to be late."

Lydia wiped away the wetness on her cheeks. "I'll drive into Mesquite and buy a test kit." She wouldn't be able to concentrate on anything until she had an answer.

"There's a Walmart on the outskirts of town," her aunt said.

"Be back shortly." Lydia climbed into her car and turned on the radio, hoping the music would drown out the panicked voices in her head. A half hour later she parked in front of the store and went inside. Just her luck that a young man was stocking the test kits in the pharmacy.

"Can I help you find something?" he asked.

"I'm looking for one of those." Lydia pointed to the First Response pregnancy test he held in his hand. She expected him to become embarrassed and move out of her way. Instead he said, "Clearblue is another popular brand." He pointed to the box on the shelf.

"Thanks, but—" Lydia gestured to the one he held "—that will be fine." He gave it to her and she made a beeline for the front of the store. The self-checkout registers were closed, so she stood in line behind a woman who'd bought a week's worth of groceries. Almost ten minutes passed before there was room to set her purchase on the counter. She opened her wallet and pulled out her debit card.

"Lydia?"

Had someone said her name? She turned and came face-to-face with... "Chantilly?"

The woman fluffed her dark curls. "I thought you'd have gone back to Wisconsin by now."

Lydia shifted sideways, trying to block the test kit from view. "The motel renovation will be done soon—then I'm heading home."

"I heard Gunner wasn't riding again until the motel reopened."

"Ma'am?" the checkout clerk said.

Lydia spun around, expecting the woman to tell her the total, but instead she held up the pregnancy kit and asked, "Do you want to use the coupon taped to the box for this purchase?"

Chantilly's gasp echoed in Lydia's ear.

"No." The clerk raised an eyebrow, so Lydia said, "Sure, go ahead."

"Is that for you?" Chantilly pointed to the plastic bag the checker had dropped the kit into.

It was on the tip of her tongue to lie, but the smug look on Chantilly's face changed her mind. "As a matter of fact, it is." Lydia walked out of the Walmart with her head held high. She waited until after she got into her car and returned to the highway before blubbering.

By the time she reached her aunt's Victorian, her tears had dried. "I'll be upstairs, Aunt Amelia."

"Take your time, dear."

Once she'd locked the bathroom door, Lydia followed the instructions on the test kit, then sat on the floor next to the claw-foot tub and counted the black and white hexagon tiles as she waited.

Her phone beeped with a text message. *Gunner*. He couldn't know what she was doing right now.

I'm at the motel. Where are you?

I'll be there in a little while.

Everything okay?

   If he only knew.

Fine.

Karl's doing electrical work. What do you want me to do?

Will you drive into San Antonio and pick up the paint for the rooms?

Text me the color info.

Will do, thanks.

   She held her breath, hoping that was the last text from him. A minute passed. Then another. And another. Finally, she relaxed.

   If she remained locked in the bathroom much longer, her aunt would check on her. She climbed to her feet and walked over to the counter. A *line* would decide her fate—two if she was pregnant and one if she wasn't.

   Lydia screwed up the courage to look at the stick, then blew out a shaky breath and returned to the kitchen. "I'm pregnant." She sat at the table and reached for her aunt's hand. Neither spoke as Lydia slowly came to terms with her situation. "I'm keeping the baby."

   "I know."

   "How?"

   "You've got the Rinehart genes in you and the Rinehart ladies never run from trouble."

   Lydia opened her mouth to confess that the urge to

run from this particular problem was powerful, but someone pounded at the back door before she could get the words out.

"What in the world is he doing here?" Amelia opened the door. "Emmett."

"Amelia." He cleared his throat. "I'm here to reassure Lydia that Gunner will marry her."

Lydia stood so fast her chair crashed to the floor.

"What are you talking about?" Amelia spoke in a calm voice.

"You gonna stand there and pretend you don't know?" Emmett said.

"Don't know what? You're not making any sense."

"Sass me all you want, Amelia, but I heard Lydia bought a pregnancy test at the Walmart in Mesquite a short while ago." Emmett's gaze traveled over Amelia's body. "Unless you've been lying about your age the past four decades and sleeping around, I don't think that test kit was for you."

"You're acting like a jackass," Amelia said. "This is none of your business." She went to close the door, but Emmett's boot got in the way.

"Anything involving my grandson is my business."

Lydia walked over to her aunt's side and faced Gunner's grandfather. "Who told you I'm pregnant, Mr. Hardell?"

"One of those bimbo girls who follow the boys around the rodeo circuit told Martha Schuler, who told Bill Packer, who called Emma Sterns, who happened to be eating in the booth next to my table at the Cattle Drive Café. Emma asked me if it was true." He raised his arms in the air. "I said I didn't know, but I'd find out soon enough."

"I assure you that I have the situation under control," Lydia said.

"You're not thinking of getting rid of the baby, are you?" he asked.

"Emmett!" Amelia slapped a palm against her chest. "You need to leave." When he didn't budge from the porch, she glared at his boot. "Now."

"Not until I know if Lydia plans to marry my grandson."

"I will not be marrying Gunner," Lydia said.

"He's the father of your baby, isn't he?"

"Yes, but that doesn't mean we have to marry." This wasn't right. Lydia should be having this conversation with Gunner, not his grandfather.

"Talk some sense into that gal." Emmett pointed at Lydia.

Amelia planted her hands on her hips. "This is between Lydia and Gunner."

"What's between Lydia and me?" Gunner climbed the porch steps, wearing his usual good-natured grin.

"You're supposed to be driving into San Antonio to pick up the paint for the motel," Lydia said.

"I thought you might like to ride along and stop for lunch at Porkies. They're known for their barbecue ribs and it's only fifteen minutes out of the way." Gunner beamed at his grandfather as if he expected the old man to congratulate him on the idea. Instead Emmett took off his cowboy hat and smacked it against his grandson's chest.

Gunner stumbled back a step. "What was that for?"

"For being stupid."

"Stupid about what?"

"Lydia's got a bun in the oven." Emmett slapped his hat against Gunner's chest a second time. "Take a wild guess who the baker is."

Chapter Nine

Gunner swallowed hard, positive he'd misheard his grandfather. Lydia couldn't be pregnant. They'd used protection—he always used protection. His heart dropped to his stomach when she refused to make eye contact.

"I'll brew a pot of coffee." Amelia grabbed Emmett's shirtsleeve and dragged him into the kitchen, then pushed Lydia onto the porch before shutting the door.

"Is it true?" he asked.

"Yes."

The one-word answer punched him in the chest. He removed his hat and shoved his hand through his hair. *Baby* bounced around inside his head, but he couldn't grasp the meaning of the four-letter word. "We used protection."

"Every time," she said.

Had one of his condoms torn and they hadn't noticed? *It's your fault Lydia's pregnant.* Of course it was his fault—he had the part B that fit into her part A. "I'm sorry." What else could he say? "What can I do?" This was the first time he'd ever been in this situation and he had no idea what was expected of him.

"I'm taking responsibility for this pregnancy, Gunner." She drew in a deep breath. "I don't expect anything from you."

"What does that mean?"

She rubbed her brow and her rosy cheeks looked as if they'd been snowed on. Gunner lunged forward and caught her around the waist, then guided her to the wicker chair in the corner. Once she was seated, he leaned against the porch rail and tried his best to keep his panic from showing. Fatherhood had never been in his plans. Oh, heck. What was he talking about? He had no plans.

He closed his eyes and tried to envision a little boy who looked like him but couldn't. He wasn't cut out to be a father. He knew it. His brothers knew it. Gramps knew it.

"Neither of us meant for this to happen." The fresh tears in her eyes ripped him apart. She'd joined a dating site because she'd wanted to settle down, marry and have kids with Mr. Perfect—not him.

"We don't have to make a big deal about this," she said.

"A baby *is* a big deal." Pregnancy hormones must have kicked in already, because she wasn't making sense. "You want us to just ignore the fact that you're pregnant?"

"Not us...*you*."

He should have been relieved that Lydia was letting him off the hook, but the churning in his gut felt like indigestion. He thought of his mother running out on their family. For months after she'd left, he'd gone to bed wondering what was wrong with him. What terrible offense he'd committed that made his mother not want to have anything to do with him. After what he'd gone through, how could he walk away from his own child? "What are you saying?"

"I don't expect you to help raise the baby. You never planned to have kids and you shouldn't be burdened with this lifelong responsibility."

She was serious. It hurt that Lydia had no faith in him. He stared into space, his fingers squeezing the handrail until his knuckles glowed white. Everyone believed he was nothing but a lazy cowboy—and until now he hadn't had a good reason to change that opinion of him.

"We'll get married," he said. Because that's what stand-up guys did—they took responsibility for their actions. Besides, his grandfather would kick his sorry butt across three counties if he didn't propose to Lydia.

"No."

"Why not?"

Her eyes rounded. "Isn't it obvious?"

"What's obvious is that you're pregnant and I'm the father."

"As much as I appreciate your offer—" she didn't act like she appreciated it at all "—you don't want to marry me."

Maybe she did know him better than he thought. "You have no idea what I want."

"You don't love me."

Love? "Who said anything about love?"

She flinched. "Why would you propose if you don't love me?"

Why were they talking in circles? "It's the right thing to do."

Lydia's mouth curved into a smile.

Was she mocking him?

"I'm afraid I'll have to pass on your gallant offer."

Her flat-out refusal stunned him. "Why?"

"Seriously?" She stared with the same sober expression his third-grade teacher, Mrs. Cunningham, had leveled at him when she'd caught him making armpit-farting noises in class.

Keeping a lid on his frustration, he said, "You're in no position to call the shots."

"Really?" Her gaze dropped to his stomach. "I'm the one who's pregnant unless you're part sea horse."

"What?"

"Male sea horses."

If being a couple weeks pregnant made Lydia talk nonsense, he couldn't imagine her jibber-jabber eight months from now. "What about male sea horses?"

"They can get pregnant." She waved a hand in front of her face. "Never mind. Just know that you're off the hook."

A lot of guys in his situation would be relieved and overjoyed to walk away from the responsibility of raising a kid, yet *he* was petitioning the mother of his child to allow him into their lives. "Most women would expect the father of their child to step up and—"

"Maybe those fathers aren't…" She rubbed her brow.

"Finish your thought." Even though he was confident he didn't care to hear it.

"Immature."

She'd gone for his jugular. He opened his mouth to protest, then snapped it closed. His father had put having a good time before his wife and kids. His mother had abandoned them for her own selfish reasons. All the good intentions in the world wouldn't trump his genetics.

As much as it pained him to acknowledge that Lydia might be right, Gunner was man enough to admit he wasn't ready to be a father. "We won't get married, then." It would be challenging enough worrying about being a good father, never mind a good husband. "But you'll need help with the baby."

"If it'll make you feel better, you can send a support check every month or whenever you're able to."

Now she was pissing him off. "I'll help you raise our child." He'd make time for his own kid.

"That'll be tough to do when you're here and I'm in Wisconsin."

He wondered if there was a chance of talking her into relocating to Stampede.

"No."

She'd read his mind, but that didn't mean he couldn't try to change hers. "Then I'll fly or drive to Wisconsin to help with the baby." And once in a while she'd visit her aunt—but who knew how many years Amelia had left before she took flight with the angels.

"There's no need for promises or assurances right now," Lydia said. "I've got this under control."

Translation... *I don't need you, Gunner.* First his mother and now Lydia. "Aside from being caught off guard by this pregnancy, how do you feel about being a mother?" he asked.

Her smile reached her eyes. "I'm ready."

He believed her, because she'd told him as much at the Singing Swine. But a baby would put a kink in Lydia's online dating plans, and that pleased Gunner more than it should have.

The back door opened and Lydia's aunt stepped outside with his grandfather. "Have you two resolved things?" she asked.

"For now," Gunner said.

His grandfather poked his hat in Gunner's chest. "When's the wedding?"

He threw Lydia under the bus. "Lydia says there isn't going to be a wedding."

"Have you gone bonkers in the head, gal?"

"Emmett, I warned you," Amelia said.

"You know what they call women who get pregnant and don't have a husband?" Emmett asked.

"Gramps…" Gunner warned.

"In case you haven't looked in the mirror lately," Amelia said, "you're old and times have changed." She placed her hand on Lydia's shoulder. "You gentlemen best be on your way."

"You really screwed up, boy." Emmett descended the steps and walked to his truck.

Gunner spoke to Lydia. "The offer's still open if you want to come with me to San Antonio to pick up the paint for the rooms."

"Thanks, but I'll stay here and rest," she said.

"See you later." Gunner hopped into his pickup and followed his grandfather through town. It wasn't until he passed the Moonlight Motel that he realized he'd left his wallet on the bed. He made a U-turn and headed back.

When he walked into room 1, Lydia's scent filled his head and for the first time he wished he'd ripped out the carpet, removed the wallpaper and the furniture, because everything reminded him of Lydia. He fell backward on the mattress and stared at the ceiling, his chest tight.

Parenthood scared the crap out of him. He had a better shot at clinging to the back of a rank bronc than being the kind of father Lydia wanted for their child. Even though the odds weren't in his favor, he'd step up and show Lydia that she and their baby could count on him.

He just had to figure out where to start.

"AUNT AMELIA, WOULD you mind if I hung out here with you a while longer after the motel renovations are finished?" Lydia stirred the oatmeal in her bowl with one hand and crossed her fingers beneath the kitchen table with the other.

"What about your decorating business?"

"I can connect with my clients using Google Chat and FaceTime." She needed to work on acquiring new business, especially now with a baby on the way, but she wasn't ready to tell her parents or cousins about her pregnancy. Lydia swallowed her oatmeal slowly, hoping her stomach wouldn't object.

"You're welcome to stay forever if you'd like."

And as long as Lydia used her family as an excuse for wanting to remain in town, she didn't need to acknowledge the truth—that she wasn't ready to say goodbye to Gunner.

"I get lonely rambling around this big house by myself." Amelia set a cup of decaffeinated green tea in front of Lydia. "But you realize, you can't keep the baby a secret forever."

Lydia blew on the hot tea. She couldn't imagine her

cousins' reactions when they heard the father of her baby was one of the notorious Hardell boys.

"How do you think your folks will take the news?"

"They'll be surprised." But Lydia's pregnancy wouldn't impact their lives. Her father and mother were dedicated to their careers. They'd attend their grandchild's birthday parties and get together on holidays, but as far as spending quality time with the child or offering to babysit—probably not.

"I'm excited about the baby." Amelia smiled. "I'd love to hear the pitter-patter of little feet running through this house again. I remember how you, Sadie and Scarlett played hide-and-seek in the closets on the second floor."

"We loved hiding out in the attic, too."

"Why don't we turn the third floor into a playroom?" Amelia clapped her hands. "And you could make one of the upstairs bedrooms into a nursery for when you visit with the baby."

Lydia's heart squeezed at the thought that her greataunt might not live long enough to see the baby grow up. Since she needed a place to hide until she was ready to answer all the how, why, where, when and who questions, she jumped on board with the idea. "I would love to convert the attic into a playroom."

"Good. What's on your agenda for today?" Amelia asked.

"Check in with Gunner and see if he's made progress painting the rooms." With Karl still working on the electrical upgrades, Lydia had planned on helping Gunner paint, but she'd grown faint from the fumes on Monday and he'd told her to keep away from the motel. It had been almost a week since she'd turned down his marriage proposal, and although he hadn't brought up the subject again, that didn't mean he wouldn't insist on helping her raise the baby. She could envision Gunner playing with their child, but when it came to discipline, she doubted she could count on his support.

"We'll discuss the attic makeover after you call Gunner."

"I'd planned to drive over to the motel and look at the rooms." Plus, she wanted to see Gunner in person, because she missed him. There, she admitted it. She missed the goofy twinkle in his eyes when he teased her. Missed the smell of his cologne when he stood close to her. Missed the way he managed to bump into her in large spaces.

She just plain missed him.

Amelia grabbed her purse and walked to the door. "Since you have plans, I'll pay Cecilia a visit. She's been lonely after Harry left to drive a load of construction material up to Oregon. We'll probably go out to supper tonight."

"Have fun." Lydia set her empty bowl in the sink, then went upstairs to brush her teeth and put on makeup. Afterward she studied the slim pickings in her suitcase and selected a blue cotton skirt and white V-neck T-shirt. She slipped her feet into a pair of low-heeled wedges and returned downstairs. Fifteen minutes later when she was confident her breakfast would remain in her stomach, she left the house.

As she pulled up to the motel, she noticed Gunner's truck parked by the office, and the door to room 6 stood open. When she got out of the car, Gunner stepped into view.

She braced herself, expecting some awkwardness

between them, but nonetheless put on a brave face. If she had to, she'd call a truce today, because she was exhausted from worrying about the future, her decorating business and telling her family about the baby. And although she would never let on, she was nervous about raising a baby alone. "Hey, Gunner." She stopped a few feet away from him. "I came by to see how things were going."

"I figured you wouldn't stay away, so I picked up a few of these at the feedstore in Rocky Point." He pulled out a red bandanna from his jeans pocket and handed it to her.

"What's this for?"

"To cover your nose so the paint fumes don't make you sick."

Lydia's heart tumbled at his thoughtful gesture.

"I sprayed it with my cologne because I know how much you like it."

She smiled, remembering the last time they'd made love and how she'd nuzzled his neck and whispered that she thought his cologne smelled sexy.

He took her hand and led her into the room. "I painted the walls in that boring white color you and your aunt picked. And I left the bathrooms alone like you said." He spread his arms wide, obviously proud of his efforts.

Lydia pressed the cloth to her nose and breathed in the warm woodsy scent, letting it go to her head before sinking into her chest, where it settled around her heart.

"What do you think?" he asked.

No drips. No paint spilled on the baseboards or splotches on the ceiling. "I'm impressed."

He tilted his head as if trying to gauge her sincerity.

"I honestly didn't think you'd do this great a job," she said.

"Painting walls is about as exciting as watching a rodeo instead of competing in one, but a guy does what a guy's gotta do…or something like that."

Lydia smiled behind the handkerchief. "It looks fantastic."

"Karl left for Mesquite a half hour ago to buy a new circuit breaker. He said he might not be back until late this afternoon." Gunner placed the lid on the five-gallon paint container and pounded it shut. "How much do you think we can charge for a night once the renovations are completed?"

"A hundred dollars. Maybe 110," she said.

"The paint fumes are going to your head. Let's get out of here." They walked to the office and he held the door open for her.

"It's nice and cool in here," she said as she passed in front of the air conditioner.

"You can give that back to me now." He nodded to the handkerchief she kept pressed against her nose.

"Sorry." She handed it over, then sniffed the air. "What's that smell?"

"Lavender and peppermint." He pointed to the rocket-shaped diffuser with mist pouring out of its top. "It's supposed to help with morning sickness." He reached beneath the counter and set out the brown bottles. "You can rub a drop of lavender against your temple or the base of your neck to help you relax when you feel uptight."

"How do you know all this?" she asked.

"I've been Googling stuff since I found out you were pregnant."

Lydia would have expected Gunner to Google how to get off the hook for an unplanned pregnancy—not ways to help the mother-to-be feel better. "That's very thoughtful of you—thanks."

"I want you to feel comfortable here." He opened the mini fridge in the corner. "This fruit-infused water should also help with your morning sickness."

Lydia squinted at the glass bottle. "What's in it?"

"Peeled ginger root and a lemon." He grabbed a plastic cup off the top of the fridge and filled it. "Tell me if it tastes any good."

She took a tentative sip. "Not bad."

He motioned to the white rocking chair across the room. "That was my grandmother's." His gaze slid to her stomach, then back to her face. "The rocking motion is supposed to calm a restless baby. If you practice now, when he's bigger and moves around more, he'll settle down after you sit in the chair."

"He?"

Gunner grinned. "Or her." He reached beneath the counter, then held up a book. *"What to Expect When You're Expecting."*

Numerous sticky notes poked out from between the pages. That he'd actually read the book impressed her, especially when they'd only just found out she was pregnant.

"You're welcome to read it when you're here," he said.

"This isn't for me?"

His face flushed red and for an instant he looked like a little boy caught misbehaving. "I can order you a copy from Amazon."

"That's okay. We can share it."

"I got you these, too." He set a box of prenatal vitamins on the counter. "In case you forget to take one before you leave your aunt's house in the morning, you'll have a supply here."

She appreciated Gunner's concern for her and the baby, but she couldn't help wondering what he was up to. Even if his interest was genuine, in a few weeks the excitement and newness of their situation would dissipate and he'd grow bored and take off rodeoing again.

"You didn't need to do this," she said.

"I wanted to." He stared at her flat stomach. "We're in this together."

No, they weren't. Lydia had to prepare herself for tackling parenthood alone. She wouldn't stop Gunner from playing expectant father, because he meant well, but she had a feeling when she really needed him, he'd be MIA.

"Now that the walls are finished, I'll start painting the trim."

"I thought the trim was in decent shape."

"Karl replaced some of the baseboards that were damaged. I've already primed them. They just need a coat of semigloss paint."

"Show me what he did." Lydia opened the door, then said, "Mind if I borrow that handkerchief again?"

Gunner handed her the cloth, then went outside. Lydia trailed behind him. With the cotton pressed firmly against her nose and Gunner's scent filling her head, she almost believed the cowboy was serious about going the distance with her and their child.

Almost.

Chapter Ten

"What are you doing here?"

At the sound of his brother's voice, Gunner glanced over his shoulder. Logan stood sock-footed in the kitchen doorway.

"I'm hungry," Gunner said.

After Lydia had left the motel last night, he'd tossed and turned in bed. At 3:00 a.m. he'd crawled out from under the blankets and driven to the ranch to scrounge up something to eat. He removed a carton of eggs and a package of sausage patties from the fridge. "You joining me?"

"Sure." Logan pulled out a chair at the table and sat. "It's Friday. Shouldn't you be on the road to a rodeo?"

Gunner had other things on his mind—like worrying about the future, Lydia and their baby. "I'm staying in town this weekend."

Logan raised his arms above his head and stretched.

"What's up with you?" Gunner asked. "You never get out of bed before five."

"I heard your truck pull up to the house."

"Sorry I woke you."

His brother waved off the apology and closed his eyes. While Logan catnapped at the table, Gunner scrambled a dozen eggs and microwaved the sausage patties, then divided the food between two plates. "You want orange juice or milk?"

"Juice."

Gunner delivered their food to the table and sat down. They ate to the sound of the ticking wall clock. These days meals were quiet at Paradise Ranch. When their father had been alive, dinnertime had been filled with boisterous jokes, laughter and teasing. He studied Logan's solemn face—it had been a long time since his brother had tried to pull a prank on him. Ever since his divorce from Beth, he was no fun to be around.

"Grandpa told me." Logan shoveled a bite of food into his mouth.

Gunner braced himself for a lecture. "It wasn't planned."

"Women today don't get pregnant unless they want to."

"Lydia's not like that. Condoms aren't foolproof." This could have happened with any of the women he'd been with in the past. He was just glad it had happened with Lydia and not one of the ditzy ladies he'd dated.

"Are you two tying the knot?"

"I offered, but Lydia doesn't want to marry me." If it had been a wild child like Chantilly or Maisy letting him off the hook, he'd have jumped for joy, but because it was Lydia—a woman who had her act together—it stung.

"I don't blame her." Logan shoveled another forkful of eggs into his mouth.

Gunner let the remark slide. He wasn't in the mood to argue. "I want to help raise our baby, but Lydia says I'm too immature."

Logan pushed his empty plate away. "I agree with her."

"Figured you would."

"You might be the best-looking Hardell, but you've half-assed your way through life, little brother."

"What's that supposed to mean?"

"Do you ever think that you might make money busting broncs if you put in the time and practice?"

"I have the motel to run."

"You only open the place if you're injured or shacking up with a buckle bunny."

"I don't bring women to the motel." Room 1 was his private sanctuary, where he could escape giggling cowgirls. Of all the women he'd had relationships with—well, flings—Lydia was the only one he'd allowed in his room.

"You do the bare minimum to get by," Logan said.

"What's wrong with the way I live? Have I ever had to borrow money from you or Gramps?" Gunner shook his head, answering his own question. "Okay, so I eat here once in a while and do my laundry on occasion. Otherwise I stay at the motel and mind my own business."

"You're twenty-seven and you've got nothing to show for it." His brother swatted the air in front of his face. "No wonder Lydia doesn't believe she can count on you. She'll have enough responsibility with her own job and caring for the baby. The last thing she needs is a freeloader."

"You cut right to the chase, don't you?" Logan's words stung, but there was some truth to them.

"You've been able to do what you've wanted all your life, Gunner."

"You're just pissed that after Dad died and Gramps fell off the wagon, you had to leave the circuit to help run the ranch."

"What do you mean, help? I run this place all by myself." Logan spread his arms wide. "I had to give up my rodeo career while you and Reid went about your lives doing what you wanted."

"I would help, but you'll just say I'm in the way," Gunner said.

"Must be nice to go through life justifying your actions so you never feel guilty."

"It shouldn't matter that I'm not a rancher like you or that I didn't join the military like Reid. That doesn't make me any less entitled to be involved in my kid's life."

"Maybe Lydia doesn't want her child's father coming and going whenever it fits into his schedule. What if she wants a steady Eddy instead of a come-and-go Joe?"

"I can be a steady Eddy." He hadn't missed a day of working on the renovations since he'd learned he was going to be a father two weeks ago.

"It's not just about holding down a job and bringing in a paycheck. It's about putting in the time. A good father puts his kids before himself."

Logan's remarks chipped away at Gunner's confidence, especially considering that their father had been a crappy role model and hadn't taught any of his sons a thing worth remembering. All the baby-book reading in the world couldn't fix his defective DNA. Points for good intentions were useless when a child's well-being was at stake, which meant he hadn't a chance in hell of winning Lydia over.

Lydia? This was about the baby, not the baby's mother.

Flustered, he checked the time on his phone. Four thirty. He might as well get started on the motel to-do list. But before he left, he remembered he'd wanted to ask his brother about their grandfather's relationship with Amelia. "Logan."

"What?"

"There's something going on between Gramps and Amelia."

"What do you mean?"

"When they're together, they always argue, which makes me think they can't stand each other, but then I caught Gramps watching Amelia walk away from him."

"What's odd about that?"

"He looked like a lovesick fifteen-year-old with his first crush."

"You must be seeing things. I've never heard Gramps say anything complimentary about Amelia."

"Maybe I imagined it." He pointed to the hallway that led to their grandfather's bedroom. "What's he been up to lately?"

"He worked out a new contract with the state highway department to mow the weeds."

"I wondered if the road was gonna get mowed this year. Looks like a jungle when you come into town."

"When Gramps found out the highway leading into Mesquite and Rocky Point had already been mowed twice this past May and Stampede got skipped over, he about blew a gasket."

Gunner grinned and walked to the back door. "Thanks."

"For what?"

"For listening." And lecturing, but he let that part go. Even though Logan complained about Gunner's lack of effort around the ranch, his brother had always looked out for him. Logan would make a great father, yet by some crazy twist of fate, Gunner would be the first Hardell brother to have a kid.

Ten minutes after leaving the ranch, he arrived at the motel, surprised to find Lydia's car in the parking lot. What was she doing up at this early hour? He'd read the pregnancy book twice from start to finish, so he knew expectant mothers needed a lot of sleep. Worried she wasn't feeling well, he entered the office and found her snoozing in the rocking chair.

Tenderness welled inside him at the sight of her—head slumped on her chest, her bare feet poking out from beneath a pair of pink-and-white-striped pajama bottoms. Her tank top was covered in tiny flamingos—whether she'd admit it or not, there was a little bit of country in the city girl.

The air diffuser and bottle of lavender oil sat on the floor near the rocker. Lydia had paid attention when he'd explained how the scented oil would help her relax. Maybe he'd impressed her a tiny bit with his knowledge.

He hated to disturb her, but if she remained in that position, she'd wake with a kink in her neck. Carefully he scooped her into his arms and carried her to his room. She stirred when he slid the key into the lock—looked him in the eye, then smiled and laid her head back on his shoulder.

He placed her in his bed, pulled the sheet over her and then turned the air conditioner on and closed the curtains before leaving the room. He returned to the office and perused the checklist Lydia had taped to the wall behind the counter. The muffled sound of a phone ringing drew his eyes to Lydia's purse on the floor by the rocker. He retrieved her purse and stowed it beneath the counter. A few minutes later her cell phone rang again. He had no business checking her phone, but it might be her aunt calling with an emergency. He rummaged through the purse and pulled out the phone. Karl had tried to call Lydia but hadn't left a voice mail message. Why would he bother her this early in the morning? He returned the contractor's call.

"Karl, it's Gunner."

"I was trying to reach Lydia."

"She's sleeping." A lengthy pause greeted Gunner's statement.

"I wanted to tell her that I won't be coming in today or tomorrow. The girls caught a stomach virus and their mother can't miss work to take care of them."

"Sorry to hear your daughters are ill."

"Lydia changed her mind about replacing the tile in all of the bathrooms and I'd planned to start removing the old tile today—"

"I can do that."

"You sure?"

"Yeah, no problem. Does it matter which room I start in?"

"Nope, take your pick."

Why hadn't Lydia told him she'd changed her mind about redoing the bathrooms?

Probably because she thought you'd volunteer to help.

"I'll take care of it. Hope your girls feel better soon."

"Thanks."

Gunner ended the call. Now what? He'd just committed to removing bathroom tiles and had no clue how to do it, but he refused to pass up the opportunity to show Lydia that he could follow through on a task. He pulled out his phone and Googled how-to videos on tiling. Twenty minutes later he entered room 6 wearing goggles. By the time he'd chiseled off half the shower tile, his shirt was soaked with sweat and he was breathing hard.

"What are you doing?" Lydia stood in the doorway, still wearing the flamingo pj's.

"Getting a jump on the bathroom demolition."

"Karl's supposed to be doing this."

"He called while you were sleeping. His daughters are ill and he has to stay home with them. I told him I'd work on the bathrooms." He chiseled off another tile.

"You don't have to do this."

"I don't want you to fall behind." He changed the subject before she kicked him off the project. "What's up with you sleeping in the office?"

She left the bathroom and he followed her.

"Insomnia," she said when she reached the door. "I'm worried about my design business. I lost Mrs. Higginson as a client after I told her I wouldn't be returning to Madison until the end of August."

He rubbed his ear, thinking he'd heard her wrong. "You're staying all summer?"

"I changed my plans."

Gunner didn't care what her reasons were for not leaving; he was just relieved he had more time to prove himself to her.

"I've got things under control the next couple of

days while Karl's gone. Why don't you try to find a new client or two right here in Stampede?"

"I doubt anyone in town is looking for a room make-over." She opened the door. "Are you rodeoing this weekend?"

She still didn't believe him after he'd told her he was taking a break from the sport until the motel was finished. "Didn't plan on it."

"You'd rather work on bathrooms than ride a wild horse and have pretty women fawn over you?"

"I admit breaking broncs is more fun than breaking tile, but as far as pretty women go..." His gaze bore into her eyes. "The only woman I want drooling over me is standing on the other side of this room."

"You don't have to pretend, Gunner." She jutted her chin. "We're too different, and if we let this become something more between us for the sake of the baby, we'll have an even bigger mess on our hands."

If he protested too much, Lydia would dig her heels in or, worse, change her mind and return to Wisconsin before the end of the summer. "Since I'm the father, don't you think we should get to know each other better?"

"I think we know each other pretty well already."

He pointed to her tank top. "I didn't know you were a fan of flamingos."

She smiled.

He set down his tools and closed the distance between them. "You better go back to your aunt's and change clothes unless you want to stay in your pj's all day." He escorted her out to the car and then opened the driver-side door for her. "Have you made an appointment with a doctor?"

"Not yet."

"You need to have blood work done to check for chlamydia, gonorrhea, hepatitis B, syphilis, cystic fibrosis, Rh factor and HIV. They might even do a urine culture and a Pap smear."

At her wide-eyed gape he winked. "Chapter two in the baby book." Then he added, "There's strawberry-lime-infused water in the mini fridge for you when you stop by next." He'd found the recipe online when he'd searched healthy drinks for pregnant women.

"What about room 1?" Lydia pointed out the windshield. "When do you plan to move out?"

He wasn't giving up his bachelor pad.

"Having six rooms to rent instead of five could be the difference between making your bills at the end of the month or not."

"I know your aunt believes the motel will be full every night once it's spruced up, but unless people have a reason to pass through Stampede, it ain't gonna happen. Besides—" he grinned "—I like room 1 the way it is."

Aside from being a bachelor pad, the room had special memories of him and Lydia making love on the bed and he wasn't about to allow strangers to tarnish those memories.

"If you've got nothing better to do tonight, you want to come watch me umpire a Little League game?" he asked.

"I guess I could tag along."

She didn't have to sound so enthusiastic. "Meet me here around five thirty. We'll grab a bite to eat before the game."

She nodded. "Call me if you run into any trouble today."

"I've got everything under control." He watched the Civic drive away, thinking he had a long way to go to win her over.

"I'LL BE UP in the attic if you need anything, Aunt Amelia." Lydia climbed the staircase to the second floor.

"I'm off to meet a friend for lunch. The Cattle Drive Café has half-price burgers on Fridays." Her aunt paused by the foot of the staircase and looked up. "Why don't you come along?"

And subject herself to strangers' stares? Everyone in town knew she was expecting Gunner's baby. "No, thanks. Since you suggested converting the attic into a playroom, I'm going to work on ideas for the space."

"You can't hide in this house forever, dear."

"I'm not hiding. Tonight I'm going to watch Gunner umpire a Little League game."

"Good. I'm glad to hear you two are spending time together."

There was little use in trying to convince her aunt that she had no intention of marrying Gunner, so Lydia saved her breath.

"I've said this before, but it bears repeating. Don't worry about money when you work on your designs."

No one knew exactly how wealthy her aunt was, but Lydia's parents surmised the older woman had a few million in investments and savings accounts.

"Make it a fun space so Sadie will want to visit with the boys."

"Us girls had just as much fun playing in the attic when it was nothing but dust and junk."

"Girls know how to use their imaginations. Boys need more direction." Amelia waved. "Have a good time tonight."

Lydia opened the door at the end of the hallway and climbed the narrow staircase to the third floor, then pulled the string hanging from the naked lightbulb in the middle of the room. She'd need to hire Karl to put in proper outlets and lighting.

As her eyes took in all the nooks and crannies, a warm tingle spread through her limbs. She fixated on the stained-glass window at the opposite end of the room and recalled how she and her cousins had pretended they were princesses trapped in a castle tower with a magic window.

She zigzagged between pieces of furniture draped with sheets—recognizing the school desks her aunt had purchased at an estate sale years ago. She tugged off the covering, then squeezed herself onto a miniature seat and imagined her little girl or boy drawing pictures.

Then her smile wilted—she couldn't think about the baby without thinking of Gunner. Last night she'd suffered an attack of insomnia—it was really a panic attack, but she preferred to call it otherwise.

She'd woken in a cold sweat but couldn't recall a thing about the nightmare except that she and Gunner had been arguing—probably about his wanting to help raise their baby. When a trip to the bathroom and a glass of warm milk hadn't helped her fall back asleep, she'd grabbed her car keys and had driven to the motel, thinking Gunner would be there. But his pickup hadn't been in the lot.

Instead of returning to her aunt's house, she'd remembered the diffuser and essential oils that Gunner had purchased and decided to see if they'd help her relax. She must have fallen asleep a few minutes after settling into the rocking chair, because the next time she'd woken, Gunner had been standing over her.

She pressed a hand against her heart, recalling the way the muscle jumped inside her chest when he had come into view. She blamed her reaction on the lavender oil, because she wasn't ready to face the truth—that she was falling in love with her baby's father.

It didn't matter how many promises Gunner made to her and the baby; he couldn't change who he was and he shouldn't have to. Her plan to protect her heart by avoiding him would never work, because the simple fact that she carried his baby entitled him to be involved in their lives. Attending the baseball game with him tonight would be an opportunity to practice shoring up her defenses around the cowboy, because it wouldn't take much effort on his part to make her fall under his spell and imagine the three of them as a forever family.

Lydia got up from the desk and stretched out on the antique fainting couch. With her eyes closed, thoughts of Gunner drifted away, replaced by images for a playroom. Her cell phone rang, interrupting her creative process.

Sadie.

Lydia wasn't ready to reveal her pregnancy to her cousin. "Hey, chica, what's up?"

"Nice to know you're still alive."

"I've been texting you since I arrived at Aunt Amelia's."

"It seems like you've been gone forever. I've missed you."

"I miss you and the boys, too. But things are busy with the motel and—"

"Lydia, I called because I need to vent."

More than happy to steer the conversation away from her, Lydia said, "I'm all ears." A loud exhale drifted into her ear. "Is it work?" The dental office where Sadie was the manager employed young hygienists who loved to gossip and the dentist had appointed her cousin the peacekeeper among his crew.

"No, this time it's my screwed-up life that's the subject of gossip."

"What happened?"

"It's Pete."

"What's going on with him?"

"He came into the dentist office yesterday and announced in front of everyone that he's moving to Baltimore."

"Why?"

"The woman he's been dating got a job offer there and he's decided to go with her and her kids at the end of July."

"What about his own job at the insurance company?"

"He said he'll look for something new once he's settled."

Poor Sadie. Pete had never held down a job for more than a year.

"He asked if I'd give him a few months' grace period on child-support payments."

"I hope you said no."

"I did, and he called me a selfish bitch in front of Dr. Michaels."

"Then the dummy should have found a job first before deciding to move with his girlfriend."

Another deep sigh came through the connection. "What's really the matter?" she asked.

"I don't know how to tell the boys."

Lydia's first thought was that the twins wouldn't care, because Pete rarely came to their soccer games and never kept his sons for a weekend at his apartment. "I doubt Tommy and Tyler will miss him."

"Maybe not, but their feelings will get hurt when they realize their father chose to be a dad to someone else's kids and not them."

"Maybe you should tell the twins that their father got a job someplace else and leave it at that."

"I would, but Pete wants the boys to visit him on Thanksgiving this year."

Uh-oh.

"I don't want to share my sons with another woman. Is that selfish of me?"

"Of course not. You've practically raised the boys by yourself. Pete never helped, even when you were married."

"Too bad the courts don't agree. They believe it's better for kids to have contact with both parents even if one is a jerk."

Lydia smiled. "I wish I could give you a hug."

"Thanks."

"Don't worry about Thanksgiving. Pete could move in with this woman and then get sick of her kids or leave her for someone else." Sadie had given her ex another chance when she'd discovered he'd cheated on her, but after the second time she'd thrown him out.

"Tell him you'll consider his request for the boys

to visit as long as he doesn't bring the subject up with them until you say it's okay."

"Good suggestion." Sadie sniffed. "You'll make a great mother someday, Lydia. You always keep your cool in tough situations, and believe me, raising kids is challenging, and then when you add an ex-husband into the mix, every decision becomes an argument."

Lydia wished she could tell her cousin she was one month pregnant as of yesterday. But it wasn't the right time.

"And why is it that Pete can date all he wants, but when I go on a date, I feel like I'm betraying the boys."

"Maybe it's better that he's moving away. Out of sight out of mind, you know?"

"If Pete had taken an active interest in his kids and had spent time with them, I'd support his move to Baltimore."

Sadie droned on about her ex's shortcomings, but Lydia wasn't listening anymore. Her thoughts had shifted to Gunner. As much as she worried he might break her heart, she was more concerned about the well-being of their baby's heart. She didn't want her child to wake up one day and hate her for having interfered in their relationship with their father. She'd pay a heavy price if she kept Gunner on the sidelines of their child's life.

"Lydia?"

"What?"

"I'm sorry. I know you've heard all this before, but if I don't complain about Pete to someone—"

"Don't apologize. I just wish he wasn't causing trouble."

"I need a vacation. Is there room for me and the boys at Aunt Amelia's house?"

Oh, no. "I'm sure she'd love to have you three visit."

"Maybe someday. When are you coming home? Not to put any pressure on you, but the boys miss seeing you at their soccer games."

"I'm not sure how much longer I'll be here," Lydia hedged.

"Shoot."

"What is it?"

"Pete pulled up to the house. Wish me luck."

"Everything will be okay. The boys have you no matter what happens."

"Thanks. I needed to hear that. Love you."

"Love you, too."

After Lydia disconnected the call, she left the attic and returned to the kitchen, where she poured herself a glass of cold water. She sat outside in the shade on the porch and stared at the oleander bushes. Was she coming down too hard on Gunner?

The phone call with Sadie was a reminder of how much children needed both parents—not just a mother. Sadie did her best to be both mother and father to the boys, but playing sports and catching frogs weren't her forte and the little tykes were missing out on the kinds of adventures only fathers could think up.

Gunner wasn't the most talented rodeo cowboy or most reliable motel manager, but in the last month he'd shown more interest in raising a child who'd yet to enter the world than Pete had shown his sons the past four years.

Chapter Eleven

"You're out!" Gunner called the third strike on the eleven-year-old who was famous in the league for swinging at every pitch no matter where it crossed the plate. While he waited for the next batter to put on his helmet, he glanced at the stands behind the chain-link fence.

Lydia sat in the middle of the bleachers next to two women who looked as if they were talking her ear off. When Lydia's head tipped back and she laughed, he forced himself to relax. He'd been worried she'd grow bored sitting on the metal seats for two and a half hours. When they'd arrived at the ballpark, they'd both eaten a hot dog. Then Lydia had taken her bottle of water and gone off to join the other parents. He'd called her back and asked for a good-luck kiss, but she'd rolled her eyes and walked away. Had he known Bobby Yonkers was eavesdropping, he wouldn't have asked Lydia for a kiss, because the adolescent mimicked Gunner's voice every time he came up to bat.

The redheaded freckled-faced teen took a practice swing in the batting circle, then grinned at Gunner when he stepped up to the plate. "Don't even think about it," Gunner said, trying to keep a straight face.

While they waited for the catcher to strap on his gear, Bobby mumbled, "Can I have a good-luck kiss?"

"Watch it, kid—the strike zone just got smaller."

The boy's chest shook with laughter. Gunner hollered at the catcher to hurry up, and when the boy crouched behind the plate, Gunner signaled the pitcher. The first ball crossed the plate high and inside, forcing Bobby to jump back to avoid being struck in the shoulder.

"Be careful, Bobby," Gunner said. "Mason's having trouble controlling his arm tonight."

Bobby backed away, took a practice swing, then choked up on the bat. The second pitch came straight down the gut, and in an attempt to bunt the ball, Bobby stepped too far forward and got hit. He dropped to his knee, clutching his arm.

Mason glared at Bobby, then threw down his glove and ran toward home plate. "He stepped in front of my pitch on purpose!"

Bobby got to his feet and threw his helmet to the ground. "Did not!"

"Did, too!"

"You suck at pitching!"

"You suck at hitting!"

Neither team's coach stepped forward to control his player, so Gunner handled the situation. "My time-out," he said. He grabbed both kids by their shirtsleeves and pulled them aside.

"Okay, guys, here's the deal. You two are the best players in this league, but every time your teams compete, you stir things up. What gives?" He glanced between the players. "Bobby?"

"He thinks he's hot shit—I mean crap."

"No more than you think you're hot crap," Mason said.

"The problem is you're both hot crap and you know it. Your parents know it. The other parents know it. And the high school coaches across the field who came to watch you know it."

"The high school coaches are here?" Mason glanced behind him. "Where?"

"See the two men wearing red T-shirts by the concession stand? The short man is the varsity coach and the taller man the JV coach. You're both good enough to make varsity when you get to high school, but if the coaches don't think you two can get along, then one of you is gonna be stuck on JV."

"Won't be me," Mason said.

"Won't be me," Bobby said.

Gunner stared at the boys. "You have a chance to be on the same team all four years of high school. You two alone could carry a team to a championship. Instead of trying to best one another, why don't you try to make each other better?"

When neither kid spoke, Gunner said, "Here's the deal. You shake and let bygones be bygones or I throw you both out of the game." He nodded to the stands. "Your parents make sacrifices twice a week so you can come out to the ballpark and have fun. You think they'll keep supporting you if all you do is fight on the field?"

"No," both boys said.

"What's your call?" Mason asked Gunner.

"Bobby takes first base." That was the only call he could make.

"Fine," Mason said. "But next time you try to bunt, wait for the ball to get closer before you step into it."

"Why? So you can bean me in the head?" Bobby asked.

"No, because my fastball drops an inch before it gets to the plate."

Bobby's eyes widened. "Okay, thanks." He took a step toward first base, then stopped and came back. He held out his hand and Mason shook it.

The parents applauded in the stands and the game continued. Bobby's team won in the end despite Mason getting his pitches under control. After shaking hands with the coaches, Gunner removed his protective vest and umpire's mask and stowed the equipment in his duffel bag, then went searching for Lydia in the stands. He didn't have to go far—she was waiting outside the visiting team's dugout.

"Is the boy who got hit by the pitch going to be okay?"

"Bobby's a tough kid. He'll be fine."

"The parents seemed awfully upset when it looked like the boys were going to start a fight."

"Mason and Bobby have been competing against each other for years. They're both vying for MVP of the league this season."

"Whatever you said calmed them down."

"You sound surprised."

Her mouth curved into a smile. "It's just that I've never seen you handle a situation like that."

"I may like to goof off and have fun as much as the next guy, but it's my job to keep the game under control and I take that responsibility seriously. You don't screw around when kids are involved."

Lydia stepped forward and kissed Gunner's cheek.

"What was that for?" he asked.

"That was for being an awesome umpire."

He chuckled. "I vote we stop by the root-beer stand on the way out of town." He took her hand and they walked off the field together, Gunner imagining that he and Lydia had just finished watching their own son play a Little League game.

"IF I'D KNOWN you could do tile work, I would have had you fix the upstairs bathroom at the ranch."

Gunner glanced over his shoulder and found his grandfather standing in the doorway late Saturday morning. "Karl's daughters were sick earlier in the week, so I volunteered to remove the old tiles in the bathrooms. It's not that hard once you watch how-to videos." He'd woken early, hoping to finish the bathroom demo in the final two rooms because Karl would be coming by later in the day to begin installing the new tiles. Gunner set aside his tools. "Lydia picked this penny round for the floor."

"That tile's from back in my day."

"It'll give the rooms a vintage feel to go along with the Western decor. This will be the San Antonio Room after the movie with the same name."

"Errol Flynn fell in love with a dance-hall girl in that flick. Is this room gonna look like a bordello?"

Gunner grinned. "We'll find out when the furniture arrives."

"When will that be?"

"Not sure."

"Dick Pence has been poking his nose in my business," Gramps said.

Dick Pence was the new mayor of Mesquite, Texas,

and he'd had nothing good to say about Stampede when it came up in conversation. "What kind of poking?"

"He wants a tour of the motel when it's finished. Ethel Porter ran into his wife at the Walmart and she said her husband was thinking of building a hotel on the south end of town."

The south end of town was fifteen minutes away from the Moonlight Motel. "He's worried Stampede will siphon off some of Mesquite's tourists."

"Only a fool would pass up a night here to stay in one of those modern, cold hotels."

Gunner wiggled his finger in his ear, positive he'd misunderstood the meaning behind his grandfather's words. The old man had opposed renovating the motel from the get-go, but now it sounded as if he was proud Stampede's only motel was going to be the talk of the area. As much as he hated Amelia Rinehart's plans to spruce up the town, the old man was beginning to see Stampede's potential.

"C'mon," Gunner said. "I'll show you what we've done outside." He closed the room door after they left, and they walked around behind the building to the cement patio with an outdoor grill and a playground.

"How much did that cost?" Gramps asked.

"It's not your money, so why do you care?"

"What happened to all the old furniture?"

"We donated it to a charity and a recycling company took the mattresses," Gunner said.

"What about painting the exterior?"

"It's on Lydia's to-do list."

"Guess it's an improvement from the dirt and weeds." Gramps fumbled for a cancer stick in his shirt pocket.

"I thought you'd have finished your birthday cigarettes by now."

"Last one. I've been saving it for an emergency." He took a long drag.

"What's the emergency?"

"Amelia hoodwinked me into taking her to the Fourth of July rodeo celebration in Mesquite today."

When the Fourth of July fell on a weekday, the town of Mesquite held their annual rodeo the weekend before. "You could have said no if you didn't want to go with her?"

"She's got something up her sleeve."

"Like what?"

"I'm guessing she's looking for more ideas to improve the town."

"Has she said anything about bringing back the Stampede Rodeo and Watermelon Festival?"

"No, but I'm betting it's on her mind."

Gunner had always enjoyed the festival and wouldn't mind seeing it reinstated. Before Lydia had become pregnant, he hadn't paid any attention to Stampede's demise—he'd been too wrapped up in his own life and rodeo. But with Lydia pregnant and him worrying how they'd raise their baby together while living apart, he admitted that Amelia's plan to bring tourists back to town and revive the economy would work in his favor if he could convince Lydia to relocate to Texas. With her decorating talents she could open a business and sell decor items along with her design services, like that famous husband-and-wife duo in Waco, Texas.

His grandfather took a final drag on the cigarette, then dropped the butt onto the ground and smashed it with his boot heel.

"Hey, no littering." Gunner tossed the butt into the garbage can next to the new grill.

"When you gonna make an honest woman out of Lydia?"

"Right now I'm just trying to find a way to convince her to let me help raise our baby." Gunner was doing everything possible to prove he was in it for the long haul with Lydia, but it was difficult to tell if he was making any progress.

"If you care about her, you'll protect her reputation."

Speaking of relationships... "Gramps, I'm going to throw this out there because it's been bugging me."

"What's that?"

"Do you have romantic feelings for Amelia Rinehart?"

His grandfather's eyes widened, then narrowed to alligator slits. "I got feelings for the woman, all right. She annoys the dickens out of me."

"The afternoon you found out Amelia wanted to spruce up the motel you ranted about her stubbornness and grandiose ways, but you let something slip."

"What's that?"

"You said you were glad nothing came of your feelings for her."

"You must have been smoking weed that afternoon."

"Were you her boyfriend in high school?"

"We dated some." Gramps's shoulders slumped. "Guess your grandmother's been dead long enough that I can confess I was sweet on Amelia."

"How sweet?"

His grandfather's mouth twitched. "We went together for almost a year."

"What happened?"

"We argued about something and then she broke up with me."

Gunner felt bad for his grandfather. "What about Grandma?"

"After Amelia married Robert, she pushed me and your grandmother together."

"Did you love Grandma?"

"Your grandmother was a good woman."

It didn't escape Gunner's notice that his grandfather hadn't answered the question. "If Grandma and Amelia were best friends, don't you think she'd approve of you and Amelia getting together now?"

The old man squirmed under Gunner's probing stare. "We're too old for that nonsense." Before Gunner could challenge him, his grandfather said, "This is the hardest you've worked since you were born."

"Is that a compliment?"

"Don't get a big head, boy."

"Speaking of impressing Lydia, I need to get back to work."

"I was hoping you'd take the day off and ride along to Mesquite with me and Amelia."

"You want me to be your wingman?"

Gramps nodded.

"But you wanted the motel finished ASAP so Amelia would get off your back."

"That was before you got her niece pregnant. Now that you're in a pickle, you need more time to woo that gal."

His grandfather was right—for a change. "Give me ten minutes to take a shower." Shoot, Lydia hadn't come by the motel in days, so she'd never know he'd left.

"YOU'VE BEEN COOPED UP inside the house for too long, dear."

Lydia kept her gaze on her laptop screen, where she was perusing children's playroom furniture. "I'm fine, Aunt Amelia."

"Fresh air will do you and the baby good."

"I got lots of fresh air a few nights ago at the Little League game."

"Gunner's been umpiring for a few years now. My friend Glenda's grandson plays in the league. According to Glenda's daughter-in-law, Gunner's great with the kids."

"He is." When Gunner had dropped her off after the game, Lydia had sat on the porch and stared at the stars, thinking he was a jigsaw puzzle and she was searching for that single piece that would connect all the others to create the whole picture. Any reservations she'd had about his commitment to their child had been laid to rest when she'd witnessed how he'd handled the squabble between the star baseball players. For a guy who claimed he'd never planned to have kids, he sure was good with them.

"You shouldn't stay home all by yourself."

Her aunt had woken on a mission—to coerce Lydia into accompanying her and Emmett Hardell to the Mesquite Fourth of July rodeo. Why the two were going together in the first place was a mystery.

Amelia removed her sun hat and placed it on the kitchen table, then perched her hands on her hips. Her determined stance pulled Lydia's attention away from her online shopping.

"The real reason I need you to come with me today is because I don't want to be alone with Emmett."

"That's no surprise. I'm amazed you two haven't come to blows over the motel renovation."

"That man is as stubborn as a mule." Amelia fiddled with the buttons on her blouse. "But his cantankerous personality isn't the reason he frustrates me." She walked over to the windows and stared at the backyard.

Lydia closed her laptop and said, "Then what is the reason?"

"I think Emmett's keeping a secret from me." Her aunt smiled at her reflection in the glass. "Unless we're arguing, he won't look me in the eye. I asked Sara about it years ago and she said I was imagining things and changed the subject." Her aunt turned away from the window.

"Maybe he never got over you breaking up with him," Lydia said.

"I don't even remember what we argued about that led me to stop seeing him." She drew in a shallow breath. "It was only a few weeks later that I ran into Robert. I told you the story about chasing the dog all the way into town and finding him with Robert." She paced across the room. "What I didn't tell you is that later that day at the supper table my father said everyone was talking about a young man surveying properties in the area for Shell Oil."

"You mean Robert?"

Amelia nodded. "When I told Sara I'd run into Robert earlier in the day, she'd suggested we doll ourselves up and go into town looking for him. We found him at the Saddle Up Saloon."

"You girls didn't get carded?"

"Nope. Robert asked me to dance and I fell hard for his three-piece suit and expensive cologne." Her aunt stared into space as if reliving the moment. "Sara left the bar early and Robert offered to drive me home. I barely made it in before my curfew because—" Amelia blinked, then looked Lydia straight in the eye "—we had sex in the backseat of his car."

Wow. Lydia hadn't seen that coming.

"He left town the next day. A month later I discovered I was pregnant."

Double wow.

"Emmett wanted to reconcile, but he didn't know I was pregnant." Her aunt wrung her hands. Even though decades had passed, the story was still difficult for her aunt to divulge. "A couple of months went by. Then Robert showed up out of the blue and offered to marry me."

"Did he say how he found out you were pregnant?"

Amelia shook her head. "I didn't ask, but I assumed it was my father. I hadn't confessed to my parents that I was pregnant, but I'd confided in Sara and I'm sure she shared the news with her mother, who in turn told mine."

"You never asked your folks?"

"I was too afraid and they never brought up the subject."

"What happened to the baby, Aunt Amelia?"

"I miscarried at three and a half months. After several more miscarriages in as many years Robert and I stopped trying."

"Oh, Amelia, I'm sorry."

"I honestly think Robert was relieved we never had children." She joined Lydia at the table. "He traveled all the time and his career was his top priority."

Lydia could only imagine how lonely her aunt had

been with no husband around and no children to keep her company.

"A few weeks before Sara passed away, she confessed that Emmett still had feelings for me and she gave us her blessing to be together."

"Did you tell Emmett about your talk with Sara?"

"No, because he spurned all my efforts to renew our friendship."

"So do you want me to come along today to keep you from punching or kissing Gunner's grandfather?"

Her aunt's cheeks flushed and Lydia caught a glimpse of what a younger Amelia must have looked like decades ago.

Emmett was a fool.

"I'll come along," Lydia said. Playing referee between the old couple would keep her mind off Gunner and the temptation to check up on him at the motel.

"I DIDN'T KNOW Gunner was joining us," Amelia said after she opened the back door and found both Hardell men standing on the porch.

Lydia's gaze roamed over Gunner. He looked like a cowboy today in faded jeans, a Western shirt and brown boots that matched his hat and her heart exhaled a tiny sigh.

"Gunner's been working hard, Aunt Amelia." Lydia stepped onto the porch. "He deserves a day off." Her pulse jumped when he winked at her.

The four walked to Gunner's truck. Emmett held the door open for Amelia and helped her into the backseat, then got in next to her. Gunner waited until Lydia climbed into the front seat, before shutting the door after her. The pickup didn't even make it to the end of the driveway before the old couple began sparring.

"Don't know why you have to go spy on another town's celebration," Emmett said.

"Your ears don't work well anymore, so I thought *seeing* what Mesquite is doing to improve their economy might help you understand my goals."

"I don't recall you putting your hat in the ring for mayor during the last election," Emmett said.

"Since you brought up the subject..."

Lydia lowered the visor and pretended to check her lipstick, all the while keeping an eye on the backseat.

"The Stampede Women's League is encouraging me to run against you in the next election."

"Bunch of nosy busybodies."

"Those busybodies helped elect you. Have you forgotten all the posters they put up around town and the fund-raiser they sponsored in order to pay for the new voting booth?"

"People could have written my name on a piece of paper and dropped it into a hat."

"This isn't the Wild West anymore, Emmett. Stampede needs to attract young families again or the town will dry up and die off."

"If you ask me, this country needs more towns like ours."

"No one asked you."

Lydia jumped inside her skin when she felt the warm touch of Gunner's fingers trapping her hand against the console between their seats. A tingling sensation traveled up her arm and spread through her chest, the intensity fueled by the memory of their lovemaking. Just because she'd kept her distance from the motel didn't mean Gunner hadn't been on her mind, especially at bedtime. At night lying in the dark with her hand resting on her belly, she'd wished with all her heart for a happy outcome to her and Gunner's situation, which right now seemed impossible when the two of them would live thirteen hundred miles apart.

Gunner waggled his eyebrows, obviously making fun of the bickering duo. Lydia laughed out loud.

"What's so funny?" Emmett asked.

Gunner saved her from answering when he turned on the radio and country music filled the cab. The backseat grew quiet and the remainder of the ride into Mesquite was made in silence with Gunner holding her hand.

After they parked at the fairgrounds, the Hardell men helped the ladies out of the truck.

"I could use a glass of lemonade," Amelia said. Emmett offered his arm and the two walked off, leaving Gunner and Lydia behind.

"So much for chaperoning," Gunner muttered.

"What do you mean?"

"Gramps asked me to come along today because he was worried your aunt would hoodwink him into making more changes in Stampede."

Lydia considered spilling the beans about why she was invited, too, but didn't think her aunt would appreciate her secret getting out.

Gunner removed his cowboy hat and set it on Lydia's head. "Now you won't burn." He pushed the rim up an inch with his fingertip. "You look like a bona fide cowgirl."

Blushing, she said, "The hat doesn't exactly go with my peasant skirt and tank top."

"Cowboy hats go with everything—didn't you know that?" He took her hand and led her toward the entrance gate. "Are you thirsty or hungry?" His gaze dropped to her waist.

"Water would be nice."

Gunner purchased two bottles of water. Then they strolled through the vendors, sampling the homemade country jams and salsas before checking out the jewelry makers and stopping to watch a man use a chain saw to carve bears out of lodge poles. When Gunner excused himself to chat with an older man, Lydia walked ahead and explored the handmade nursery furniture at another booth.

"This is lovely," she said, examining the crib and matching cradle.

"My husband had a fit when I insisted on painting the pieces white instead of staining the wood."

"The white gives it an airy, modern feel even though the design is vintage." Lydia smiled. "The best of both worlds."

"My thoughts exactly." She held out her hand. "I'm Rachel."

"Lydia. Nice to meet you."

"Are you shopping for nursery furniture?"

"I will be."

Rachel beamed. "Congratulations. When are you due?"

The question caught Lydia by surprise and she stumbled over her answer. "Oh, not for a while." She ignored Rachel's puzzled expression and examined a dresser.

"We could paint that to match the crib and the cradle," Rachel said. "And there's a toy chest included in the set."

"Could your husband make a rocking horse?" Lydia pictured a miniature cowgirl or cowboy riding the toy horse.

"We do custom orders." Rachel held out a business card.

"Do you ship out of state?"

"It would be expensive. You might be better off renting a U-Haul and driving the furniture to wherever you live."

"I'll think about it. It was nice talking to you." It wasn't until she walked past several more vendors that she realized she hadn't asked the cost of the furniture—not that it mattered. She couldn't afford to buy anything until she landed a few new business accounts.

"Sorry about that," Gunner said when he caught up with her. "Joe used to rodeo with my father."

"Your dad rodeoed, too?"

"Yep." He guided her away from the crowds to a bench in the shade near the game booths. How had he known that she needed to sit down?

"Dad was pretty good at rodeo when he wasn't drinking or screwing around behind our mother's back." He cast a sideways glance at her. "Gramps is an alcoholic, too."

"Aunt Amelia told me."

"Hopefully your family genes will trump mine—" he nodded at her stomach "—and our little one won't be as rough around the edges as their father."

Our little one. There Gunner went again using words that conjured up images of family—a three-person family.

"Do you and your brothers keep in touch with your mother?"

He shook his head. "She cut her ties with us when she left my dad." Gunner's comment sounded nonchalant, but his muscles tensed, convincing her that he was more affected by his mother's abandonment than he let on. "I know where she lives," he said.

"Have you visited her?"

He shook his head. "Gramps would be upset if he found out I'd kept tabs on her. He doesn't blame her for walking out on my dad, but he won't forgive her for leaving us kids behind."

"Do you know why she didn't stay in touch with you and your brothers?"

"She married a widower with two daughters."

The woman sounded heartless, but she sensed Gunner was accepting of the situation. "A lot of people in your position would hate their mother for abandoning them."

"It takes more energy to hold a grudge than to move on."

"But..."

"What?" he asked.

She was sticking her nose where it hadn't been invited. "Never mind." Maybe his mother leaving and his father's womanizing had convinced Gunner marriage wasn't worth the effort. "I need to use the restroom."

He pointed to a brick building across from the game booths. "Take your time. I'll wait here."

Once inside the restroom, Lydia splashed cool water on her face. Why had she asked about Gunner's family history?

Because you're searching for a reason to keep him at a distance.

Was she?

Hasn't he shown you the past couple of weeks that he can be serious and dependable when he wants to be?

Gunner had been up early working at the motel every day this past week—she knew so because Karl had phoned and explained that Gunner was removing the bathroom tile while he'd remained at home, taking care of his sick daughters. And seeing how he handled the teens at the Little League game and then learning that he'd forgiven his mother all made it more difficult to hold on to the belief that Gunner wasn't serious enough to be a father.

After she used the facilities, she washed her hands and left the restroom only to skid to a stop when she saw Gunner and a little boy standing at the dart-throwing booth. Lydia scanned the area but didn't see the boy's mother anywhere.

She hid in the shadows and watched as Gunner crouched down and spoke to the boy, who then pointed to a stuffed panda bear hanging among an array of animal prizes. Gunner dug into his pocket and then handed the employee money in exchange for darts. The boy jumped up and down as Gunner made a big production of winding his arm, squinting at the target and shuffling his feet.

Gunner threw the first dart and it hit the bull's-eye. The boy squealed. Gunner went through his goofy routine again, then threw the second dart. Another bull's-eye. The game worker held up a medium-size teddy bear, but Gunner waved it off. The little boy looked unsure as Gunner prepared to throw the final dart. When it landed in the center again, the kid danced in circles.

Gunner accepted a giant panda from the worker

and handed it to the kid just as the little guy's mother raced up to them. After a quick exchange with Gunner, the mother hugged her son, obviously relieved to find him after he'd wandered off. She took the panda, then clasped her son's hand. As they walked away, the boy glanced over his shoulder and waved.

Maybe it wasn't up to Lydia or Gunner to decide if he'd make a good father.

Maybe it was up to their child.

Chapter Twelve

"You sure you're not hungry?" Gunner couldn't figure out why Lydia was so quiet after she'd returned from the restroom.

"I'm fine. I ate a second breakfast this morning."

"I can probably guess what happened to the first one." He rubbed her back in sympathy, grateful for an excuse to touch her. He missed their lovemaking, which wasn't a surprise, since they'd hit it off in bed. But what did shock him was that he missed her hanging around the motel monitoring him. He loved watching the tiny wrinkle move between her eyebrows when she concentrated and the way she nibbled her lip right before she changed her mind.

He just plain missed Lydia, which was a first for Gunner. He couldn't recall any woman occupying his thoughts every waking moment.

"I tried eggs and toast this morning." She peeked up at him. "Tasted great going down, not so great coming up."

"What was your second breakfast?"

"Oatmeal."

"Exciting." He slipped his arm around her waist and guided her away from a group of teenagers walking with their heads down and eyes on their phones. The rodeo was set to begin soon, so he steered them toward the grandstands.

"When do you plan to see a doctor?" he asked.

"I'll visit my OB-GYN when I return to Madison."

Lydia had said *Madison*—not *home*. It was a tiny slip, but he hoped it meant she was warming up to Stampede. "Have you told your parents?"

Her head snapped in his direction. "No. Who have you told?"

"Gramps spilled the beans to Logan, but I doubt he told Reid unless he called him after he got Reid's check."

"Check?"

"Each month Reid sends a thousand dollars home. Guilt money because he doesn't want to help Logan run the ranch." Gunner didn't want to talk about his brother. "Have you picked up any new clients in town?"

"A couple of Aunt Amelia's friends contacted me to do small projects, but I think my aunt coerced them to ask for my services." Lydia smiled. "I offered them decorating ideas free of charge and the ladies said they'd recommend me to their friends and family."

"What else are you doing to keep busy at your aunt's house?"

"I'm turning the third-floor attic into a playroom."

The word *playroom* caught his attention.

"My cousins and I used to hide up there and play for hours when our families visited Aunt Amelia each summer."

"That's a lot of work for a space that won't be used very often," he said.

"Aunt Amelia is hoping Sadie will visit with the twins and then I'll be coming back here with the baby."

Maybe in time one of Lydia's visits would become a permanent move.

"Hey, Gunner!"

A rodeo buddy Gunner recognized approached and he held out his hand. "How you doing, Jake?"

"Good." He glanced between Gunner and Lydia. "Why aren't you riding today?"

"Taking a break from the circuit." He pulled Lydia close to his side.

"Lydia, this is Jake Monahan. He cowboys for the Los Lobos Ranch and rides bulls for fun."

Jake tipped his hat. "Heard you're fixing up the Moonlight Motel."

"Lydia's the project designer. You should stop by and check it out," Gunner said.

"When you gonna get back to riding broncs?"

"I'm not sure." Gunner hadn't yet talked to his grandfather about the possibility of hiring a part-time employee to run the motel when he was off rodeoing.

"Since you're on vacation today, do you mind helping me in the chute?" Jake asked.

"Where are your brothers?" Jake was a triplet and his brothers, Seth and Elliot, also competed in rodeo.

"They're fixing fence." Jake grinned. "They don't want to admit they're getting too old to tangle with rough stock. Besides, they're afraid I'll show them up."

"Wish I could help, but—"

"You don't mind me borrowing Gunner for a few minutes, do you?" Jake stared at Lydia.

"Of course not."

"You sure?" Gunner asked.

"I'll wait over there." She pointed to an out-of-the-way spot behind the chutes.

Jake spoke to Lydia. "Gunner might not be a great rodeo cowboy, but he's the guy you want by your side before the chute opens and all hell breaks loose."

Gunner appreciated the backhanded compliment but doubted it would mean much to someone who didn't understand the sport.

"I drew Widow's Peak and I don't know a thing about the animal except that no one's gone the distance with him." Jake tugged his riding glove on.

"Then play it safe," Gunner said. "Stay low and keep your head down." He climbed the chute rail and stood at the bull's head as Jake slid onto its back. "Remember, nothing flashy."

Jake wrapped the rope around his hand, then undid it and tried again.

"Not too tight on the wrap. You don't want him tearing your arm from the socket." Gunner had ridden a few bulls early in his career, but after a second concussion he'd switched to broncs—not that it was less dangerous, but few horses had that killer instinct like rodeo bulls.

"The bull's back left leg is twitching," Gunner said. "I'm betting he turns left after he clears the chute."

"Got it." Jake nodded, signaling he was good to go. The chute opened and Widow's Peak did exactly as Gunner predicted—he spun left before his first buck. Jake hung on for seven seconds, his body whipping in the wind like a wet piece of rawhide. When the bull decided he'd had enough, he twisted his back end in mid-buck and Jake catapulted into the air. The moment he hit the ground, he rolled to his right to avoid a stomping, then scrambled to his feet and raced to the chute.

"Sweet ride, Jake. You almost had him," Gunner said.

"You called it right. You can read a rank bull like nobody's business, but you sure can't ride 'em."

Gunner chuckled. "If I ever solve that part of the equation, then you'd better watch out." He glanced over his shoulder and caught Lydia talking to a familiar-looking woman holding a little girl on her hip. "See ya around, Jake." Gunner dodged a stroller and a fast-walking couple to catch up to Lydia.

"Hey, Shannon," he said to the brunette.

"Howdy, Gunner." Shannon flashed her trademark beauty-pageant smile that had won her Miss Mesquite Rodeo in high school.

"Who's this?" He smiled at the little girl—a miniature version of her mother.

"This is Annabelle. She turns three tomorrow."

"Happy birthday, Miss Annabelle." Gunner winked and the child giggled. He motioned to Lydia and opened his mouth, but Shannon cut him off.

"We introduced ourselves." Shannon smiled at Lydia. "Don't worry. I didn't tell her about all the trouble you caused in high school." Shannon turned to Lydia. "Gunner asked me out every Monday in English class our sophomore year, but Daddy would have had a fit if I'd dated a Hardell boy."

The child wiggled like a fish on a hook and Shannon set her on the ground. Annabelle squatted in front of Gunner and traced the stitching on the top of his cowboy boots. "Pretty fancy boots, huh, Annabelle?" When the little girl looked up, Gunner said, "Wanna dance?" He lifted her up and set her feet on top of his boots, then stepped forward and back. Annabelle giggled.

"We better get going. Annabelle's father promised to show her the horses." Shannon smiled at Lydia. "It was nice meeting you." She took her daughter's hand. "Good luck with the motel, Gunner." The mother and daughter disappeared into the crowd.

"Let's grab lunch." Gunner escorted Lydia to the Burger Shack. She ordered a cheeseburger and fries and another bottle of water, then waited at a table in the shade for Gunner to bring their food. After he set the tray on the table and joined her, they ate in silence.

When Gunner finished his burger, Lydia spoke. "You seem at ease around children."

He popped a fry into his mouth. "It's easy to have fun with kids when you're not responsible for them and don't have to worry about their well-being."

His comment worried Lydia. Sure, he claimed to want to be a part of his child's life, but was he going to leave her with all the tough decisions a parent confronted when raising a child? It wouldn't be fair if he had all the fun but none of the liability. She bit into her burger, chewing until she was sure she could swallow past the lump in her throat. Gunner would never be her Mr. Perfect, but it was time she faced the truth—she was in love with him.

On the bright side—if there was a bright side— loving Gunner wouldn't be for naught. One day when their child asked if she'd loved their father, with a clear conscience she could answer yes, she had...and maybe still did.

"Is there anything else you want to do while we're here?" he asked.

"How about a walk through the livestock barns? I'd love to see the animals."

He nodded to her half-eaten burger. "Are you sure you can stand the smell?"

"On second thought maybe we should sit in the shade of the grandstand and watch the rest of the rodeo." And she'd pretend they were a couple until it was time to leave Stampede for good.

"I DIDN'T EXPECT to see you today." Gunner placed the caulk gun on the bathroom counter Monday morning, then gestured at the shower wall. "I wasn't sure I'd like the white subway tile, but it's growing on me."

Lydia had debated using different colors but had decided to keep the bright, clean look consistent in all the bathrooms. "You're doing a nice job. Thanks for helping Karl with the tiling."

"I made a couple of mistakes, but Karl fixed them for me, so you can't tell."

"Without your efforts we'd have fallen way behind." Karl had been forced to cut back on his hours after his daughters had been diagnosed with strep throat and had to stay home from day camp. Lydia had sympathized with the single father and she worried how she'd handle a similar situation if her own child became ill and she had to work.

"This handyman stuff is kind of growing on me." He grinned. "Don't get me wrong—rodeo is still more exciting than installing a new faucet, but it's nice to know I can do some minor repairs around the motel if they crop up in the future."

"And you have Karl's number now if you need a professional." She glanced away from his face. She was going to miss Gunner's teasing brown eyes. "I stopped by to tell you that the furniture and accessories are being delivered at the end of the week." It was only the middle of July, but her plan to remain in Stampede the entire summer had taken a detour after the Mesquite Fourth of July rodeo. "Will you be around at the end of the week to help Karl hang the wallpaper in each room?"

"Why wouldn't I be?"

"The renovations are almost finished." She shrugged. "I thought you'd want to get back to riding broncs."

"My only plan this weekend is to tackle the exterior."

She waved a hand. "I hired Smith Painting and Drywall in San Antonio to paint the motel. The owner is driving down tomorrow to look over the property."

"I can do it for the cost of the paint."

"There's more involved than just rolling on a new color. There are a few places where the stucco needs repair and it has to be taken care of properly or you'll have mold problems in the future, which could cost a lot of money to repair." She walked out of the room and Gunner followed. "See?" She pointed to the corner of the building, where there was evidence of water damage.

"I never noticed that," Gunner said.

"The owner of the company, Brett Smith, provided several references, which all checked out. Plus he's been in business over thirty years and guarantees his work." Lydia trusted the company to do a good job.

"What's next after the bathrooms and wallpaper?" he asked.

"Room 1 still needs to be renovated."

Gunner opened his mouth to protest and she cut him off. "I know, you want to keep that room for yourself, but you'll be glad it's available to rent when this place fills up during the summer months."

"Your aunt is the only one who believes the Moonlight Motel will be a hit with tourists. We'll be lucky if we rent one room a week during the summer."

She didn't want to argue with Gunner, so she dropped the subject.

"Karl will be by on Friday to install the laminate wood flooring in the office."

"What happens after you've got everything checked off your to-do list?"

Talk about a loaded question. "I hand this beautiful motel back to you to run."

"I meant what are your plans to keep busy the rest of the summer?"

"About that…" Lydia resisted squirming under his steady gaze. "As soon as I finish converting my aunt's attic into a playroom, I'm returning to Wisconsin."

The muscle along his jaw clenched. "You said you were staying for the summer."

"After you asked about making a doctor's appointment, I decided it was a good idea. I'm seeing my ob-gyn the last Monday of the month."

His gaze shifted to the wall over her shoulder and the muscles along his jaw pulsed with an effort to keep his anger in check. She didn't want to leave town with Gunner mad at her.

"I'll call you after the appointment and let you know how it went."

He nodded but didn't say a word.

"I'll be at my aunt's. Call if you need anything."

"Lydia." He opened his mouth, then snapped it closed and turned away.

It took all her resolve to coax her feet toward her car. Eyes stinging, she drove to her aunt's house, where she found a note on the kitchen table. *Gone for the day. Be back before supper. Love, Amelia.*

Blurry-eyed, Lydia sat down and pulled up her account on SavvyMatch.com. She had three new matches waiting for her to view. She clicked on TrueBlueTodd and pushed Gunner's image to the back of her mind. Like the others on the dating site, Todd checked off every box on her husband must-haves.

She clicked on Edward1224 and then Jim345. All three were perfect matches, but the tears still dripped down her cheeks. She doubted the men would want to date her when she told them she was pregnant.

Why did she have to go and fall in love with a man who was so wrong for her? Who didn't check off one box in her must-have column?

Lydia wished with all her heart that Gunner had always intended to eventually marry and have a family, but those hadn't been his plans. She knew he'd marry her for the baby's sake, but she didn't want to wake up each morning to the reality that an unplanned pregnancy had pushed them together.

If they married, she wanted it to be because Gunner loved her, not because he felt obligated for the sake of their baby or to please his grandfather. He could still be a father to their child and she'd do everything possible to keep him involved in their lives, but she loved him too much to allow him to sacrifice himself.

Thirty minutes later she had pinged several new

profiles—divorced men with children—but a splitting headache demanded she take a nap and she retreated upstairs.

GUNNER SAT ON the bed in room 1, where he'd retreated after Lydia left the motel an hour ago. He wasn't happy she was leaving Stampede before the end of the summer, but he wasn't sure what he could do to change her mind. The sound of a pickup caught his ear and he stepped outside. Karl Schmidt pulled into the lot.

"Hey, Gunner. Since I was in the neighborhood, I thought I'd stop by and make sure I have the right measurements for the flooring."

Gunner met him at the office door. "Need help?"

"I think I've got it." Schmidt stepped inside and glanced around. "Is Lydia here?"

"She left a short while ago."

"Is she at her aunt's house?"

"I think so. I'm heading over to Amelia's. You want me to give her a message?"

"I've got a couple extra boxes of flooring and wondered if she wanted me to use it in the hallway behind the office."

"I'll ask her," Gunner said.

Schmidt fiddled with the tape measure for a few minutes, then shoved it back into his pocket. "Okay, well, guess I'll be going."

"See you later." Gunner locked the office, then hopped into his truck and drove through town. Lydia's Civic sat in her aunt's driveway, but Amelia's Thunderbird was missing from the garage. The eighty-five-year-old woman sure got out a lot.

He knocked on the back door. No answer. He turned

the knob and the door opened. When he entered the kitchen, he noticed Lydia's laptop on the table, a glass of water sitting next to it. "Lydia?"

Silence.

He walked down the hallway looking inside each room—empty. He stood in the foyer gazing up the staircase, wondering if she was resting or working in the attic. He listened for noises, but all was silent, so he backtracked through the house, not wanting to disturb her. On his way to the door his thigh bumped the edge of the kitchen table and the laptop screen popped on, revealing the SavvyMatch.com website.

Things between them were a mess, that was for sure, but Lydia was having *his* baby. Why was she online looking to date other men right now?

He resisted the impulse to sit down at the table and scroll through her account, but that didn't mean he couldn't view Ted115's profile on the screen. The guy looked like a dweeb with short hair and long sideburns. Gunner scanned the man's bio. *Single dad looking forward to having more kids someday.*

Single dad? Now that Lydia was pregnant, was she looking for a potential husband who was already a father?

Gunner stared into space, envisioning another man helping to raise his child. He'd proposed to Lydia, but she'd let him off the hook—shouldn't he be relieved that his only responsibility would be to his child?

So why did it feel like someone had walked across his chest wearing spurs?

Chapter Thirteen

"You just going to sit here and drink yourself into oblivion on this fine Tuesday afternoon?"

Gunner stiffened when his grandfather's voice drifted into his ear. "You're not supposed to be in a bar."

Gunner and two other patrons in the Saddle Up Saloon had planted their backsides on stools three hours ago and none of them were in a hurry to leave.

The bartender pointed to Gunner's grandfather. "Water or coffee, Emmett?"

"Coffee, JB." Emmett nudged Gunner's elbow. "How old do you think he is?"

"Looks as old as you." JB's long hair was silver now, but he wore it in the same ponytail that he'd sported when he'd served Gunner his first legal drink way back when.

Emmett nodded his thanks after JB placed a mug of hot coffee in front of him. "You making an art project?"

Gunner ignored the question and continued building his confetti pile made out of a shredded beer label.

"Amelia said Lydia left town this morning."

"Yep."

"She say when she's coming back?"

"Nope."

"Did you ask her?"

Gunner glared at his grandfather. "I didn't see her."

"Then how'd you find out?"

"Lydia sent me a text." But not until she'd stopped for gas in San Antonio. Just far enough away that Gunner couldn't chase her down and persuade her to change her mind.

The door opened and Logan strolled in. "Shouldn't you be out chasing cows?" Gunner asked when his brother sat next to him.

"I would be, but Gramps left me a note saying you went AWOL and I was to head into town to look for you." Logan caught JB's attention and said, "I'll take a coffee."

"I haven't been AWOL. I've been right here since noon," Gunner said.

The door opened again, sending a flood of bright sunlight into the bar. Karl Schmidt waltzed in and headed straight for the group.

The one place Gunner had hoped to lick his wounds in private was turning into a gentlemen's coffee klatch.

"You want a cup of joe, too?" JB asked Karl when he delivered Logan's mug.

"Sounds good, thanks." Karl took the seat next to Logan.

JB placed an empty mug in front of Karl, then set the pot on the bar. "Pour your own refills."

"Why are you here, Schmidt?" The fact that Lydia hadn't even waited around a few days to see the office flooring installed and the furniture set up in the rooms told Gunner how badly she'd wanted to skip town.

"Lydia's not answering her phone," Karl said.

"She went back to Wisconsin," Gunner said.

Karl blew on his coffee. "I thought she was staying for the summer."

Emmett poked Gunner. "Dumbass here chased her off."

"I didn't chase anyone off."

His grandfather made a rude noise. "You didn't convince her to stay, did you?"

"Is something going on between Lydia and Gunner?" Karl spoke to Logan.

"Just a baby, is all."

Karl choked on his sip of coffee. "A baby?"

Gunner nodded. Everyone else in Stampede knew Lydia was pregnant; how had the contractor missed hearing the news?

"Well, shoot." Karl's mouth turned down at the corners. "I was thinking about asking Lydia out. Are you two getting married?"

"I told Gunner to propose, but—"

"I proposed. She doesn't want to marry me." Gunner might as well tell the truth before the town gossips came up with their own tale. "Lydia's using an online dating site called SavvyMatch.com and I'm not the match she's looking for."

"What's a dating site?" Emmett asked.

"It's like Facebook. Only, you sleep with your friends," Logan said.

"You're a fool, Gunner, if you let Lydia slip away." Karl took another sip of coffee, then threw a dollar on the bar. "If you speak to Lydia, tell her I should have the new baseboards in the office painted by the end of next week."

"I'll paint them," Gunner said. He needed something to keep his mind off Lydia.

After Karl left the bar, Logan stood. "Let's go."

"Go where?" Gunner said.

"I ran into Amelia when I stopped at the motel on the way into town."

"What was she doing out there?" Gunner asked.

"Same thing as me—looking for you. I promised I'd bring you by her place when I found you."

"I don't want to talk to the old biddy," Gunner said.

Emmett banged his fist on the bar. "Watch how you speak about Amelia."

"All you do is argue with the woman," Gunner said. "What are you defending her for?"

"Yeah, Gramps," Logan said. "You don't even like her."

"I never said I didn't like her."

"You've got a weird way of showing your affection for her, then." Logan pulled Gunner off the stool. "I have better things to do. Let's get this over with."

Emmett left a twenty on the bar. "Wait for me."

The three of them climbed into Logan's truck and drove over to Amelia's house. The older woman was sitting on her front porch waiting. "What are you doing here, Emmett?" she asked.

"He was drinking at the bar with Gunner," Logan said.

"Drinking?" Amelia's eyes rounded.

Emmett smacked his hat against Logan's back. "Coffee."

Gunner pressed his mouth into a thin line and braced himself for a verbal lashing from the old woman.

"Do you love my niece?" Her blue eyes stared daggers at Gunner.

Love? Gunner didn't know the first thing about real

love. The only love he'd known in his life had been from a mother who'd walked out on him and his brothers and a father who'd put booze, cheating on his wife and rodeo ahead of his sons. Add in an ex-sister-in-law who'd left Logan in the dust, and yeah, Gunner knew about love— just not the kind Lydia's aunt was getting at. "I don't know, ma'am," he answered honestly.

Amelia's eyes narrowed. "Any upstanding man would offer to marry the woman he got pregnant."

"I offered my hand again, but Lydia turned me down again." Gunner grimaced. "I'm not the kind of husband she's looking for." He'd been busting his backside trying to prove to Lydia that he was responsible enough to be their baby's father, all the while stupidly believing that she'd remain single. It hadn't occurred to him that sooner rather than later she'd want to make a life with another man.

Amelia's eyes sliced to Emmett before returning to Gunner's face. "Then you must convince Lydia that her tastes have changed and you are just what she needs."

If Gunner was committed to his child, wasn't he just as committed to Lydia even if they weren't married? He hated that he felt compelled to defend himself. "I gave up rodeo and did everything Lydia asked me to do and then some."

Amelia rolled her eyes. "Lydia's not going to marry you for the baby's sake or because you followed her to-do list for the motel." Amelia grasped Gunner by the shoulders and stared him in the eye. "You must make her believe she needs to marry you for *her* sake."

Instead of proving he'd be a good father to their child, Gunner should have been proving he'd be a good husband and life partner to his child's mother.

He closed his eyes and envisioned the future the way he'd always planned—single and with few responsibilities. It seemed like a lifetime ago that he was living the dream; then the dairyland princess had crashed into town, changing that dream.

Before it was too late and some SavvyMatch dweeb claimed her, he had to convince Lydia that good-time Gunner was her perfect match.

"EVERYTHING LOOKS GREAT, LYDIA." Dr. Hernandez wrote on her prescription pad, then tore off the sheet of paper and handed it to her. "But your blood work shows you're a little anemic. Take this until I see you again. Then we'll recheck your iron levels."

"Thank you, Dr. Hernandez."

The doctor paused at the door. "When you make your appointment for next month, my nurse will give you information on birthing classes."

After the door shut, Lydia's smile slid off her face. She changed out of her gown and back into her clothes, then slipped her feet into her sandals. With every passing day, Lydia was growing more excited about being a mother, but the tiny thrill was dampened by the circumstances responsible for this momentous occasion—and the fact that Gunner wasn't here to share the moment. When she'd imagined herself having a baby, she hadn't been alone.

She zigzagged her way through a maze of hallways to the waiting room, where she stopped at the desk and made her next appointment and received a handful of baby literature, which she stuffed into her purse. After thanking the receptionist, she turned to leave but froze when the door opened and Gunner walked in.

The waiting room grew still—even the phone stopped ringing. Lydia looked her fill, her heart thumping hard at the sight of Gunner in faded jeans, a Western shirt and a cowboy hat. She wasn't the only one drooling over the cowboy—every big-, medium- and small-bellied woman appeared mesmerized by him.

When Gunner's gaze landed on Lydia, the guarded look in his eyes softened. She'd left Stampede only seventy-two hours ago and had missed him every single second of that time. She met him at the door. "You remembered I had a doctor's appointment today."

He removed his hat and shoved his fingers through his hair. "I got a flat tire outside of Rockford or I would have been here two hours ago."

She took his hand and led him to the elevators. After they stepped inside and the doors closed, he asked, "What did the doctor say?"

"Everything is fine."

His eyes skipped across her face and landed on the button panel. He was nervous. "Do you have time to grab a bite to eat?" she asked.

"You pick the restaurant."

"There's leftover spaghetti at my apartment."

The elevator doors opened and they walked out to the parking lot and stopped at her Civic. "I'll follow you," he said.

Lydia started the car and watched Gunner climb into his pickup. In a few minutes she'd learn if he'd come because of the baby or if he was here because of her.

He's here, isn't he? Does it matter why?

Lydia's stomach turned somersaults all the way home and up the flight of stairs to her second-floor apartment. "I owe you an apology," she said after closing the door behind him. She set her purse on the couch and walked into the kitchen.

Gunner stopped in the doorway and leaned a shoulder against the jamb. "Apology accepted."

She removed the bowl of homemade spaghetti sauce from the fridge and placed it on the counter, then faced him. He was letting her off the hook for leaving town before the motel was finished. Before they'd set up a game plan for the future. Before they'd said goodbye. "This is a bigger mess than the motel renovations, isn't it?"

"I wouldn't call a baby a mess."

"You know what I mean." She added olive oil to the frying pan, then dumped leftover noodles into it. "You never wanted children."

"Either way, I'm still our baby's father."

"I know." She poured the leftover sauce on top of the noodles and stirred the food, then turned down the heat. "I have water or—" she poked her head inside the fridge "—beer, diet cola, milk and orange juice."

"I didn't know you drank beer."

"I don't." She kept it on hand just in case she invited a date back to her apartment for a nightcap, which hadn't happened in over a year. "On second thought the beer's probably expired."

"Water's fine." Gunner pulled a chair out at the bistro table and sat.

Lydia prepared their plates, the heat of his stare burning her back. He made her nervous. He hadn't driven all this way just to find out how her doctor's appointment went. If she'd known he'd planned to visit, she could have prepared herself. Hoping to buy a little time to get her nerves under control, she steered the conversation in a different direction. "I know what you're thinking."

"What's that?"

"I'm a professional designer, so why is my apartment boring."

His gaze roamed around the room. "I wasn't thinking that, but now that you mention it…"

"Because I work out of my apartment, I keep it as sparse as possible so my tastes don't influence the designs I create for my clients."

"If you decorated your place, what would it look like?"

"A cottage."

"I would have guessed modern or contemporary. What does *cottage* look like?"

"Cottage is more a frame of mind. It's laid-back with blended styles of furniture and ordinary treasures. My rooms would be humble, unpretentious and full of heart."

He grinned. "That sounds like something a designer would say."

Embarrassed that she'd carried on, she set their plates on the table.

"This smells great. Is it homemade?"

She nodded. "There's a farmers' market a few blocks away where I buy my fruits and vegetables."

Gunner waited for Lydia to take the first bite before digging into his meal. The cowboy had better manners than most of the men she knew. They ate in silence, Gunner scraping his plate clean.

He leaned back in his chair. "What did you find out at the doctor's appointment?"

"I'm a little anemic." When he frowned, she said,

"It's nothing to worry about yet. She gave me a prescription for an iron supplement."

"Do you have a due date?"

"Around April 4."

"Maybe the baby will be lucky and arrive on April Fools' Day."

"You would see that as a bonus." She pictured Gunner playing all kinds of pranks every year on their child's birthday and the little tyke loving it.

"Did Karl get the new flooring installed in the office?" she asked.

"It's done. And the owner of Smith Painting and Drywall showed up Friday afternoon to look over the property. His crew is supposed to start today."

"Who's watching over the motel?"

"Gramps and Amelia are manning the motel office until I get back."

Lydia raised an eyebrow.

Gunner chuckled. "I'm sure they'll provide plenty of entertainment for the painting crew." His face sobered, and he leaned his elbows on the table. "I should have warned you that I was coming."

"I'd say we're even, since I didn't tell you I was leaving...until I'd left."

"I'm here because I want to make sure you and the baby are okay."

Lydia's heart sighed at the sincere tone in his voice. He cared about her and their child. He'd never planned on being a father, but he wasn't dodging his responsibility.

Gunner's not running—you are.

"We're having an open house this weekend to show off the motel remodel. Your aunt's hired a catering company and a local band." His gaze pinned her. "Will you come back for the celebration?"

"I don't know if that's a good idea." The drive from Texas to Wisconsin had given Lydia way too much time to think. With each passing mile she'd felt as if she'd left a part of herself behind in Stampede. She blamed her pregnancy hormones in order to avoid facing the truth—that the dusty little town had grown on her.

But most of all she'd missed Gunner the second her car had left her aunt's driveway. Missed him more than she'd ever imagined. And it scared her silly, because they had little in common.

You share a baby—that's what matters most.

"If the motel takes off, the entire town will have you to thank," he said.

"Without my aunt, the motel never would have gotten a face-lift."

"You should be there, Lydia."

She carried their plates to the sink. "I just came up with the design. You and Karl did most of the work."

Gunner left his seat and approached Lydia. He took her hands in his and stared into her eyes. "We're both navigating our way through this baby thing, but I've been thinking…"

Her breath caught when he brushed the hair from her eyes and his fingers lingered against her cheek.

"I want to tackle parenthood with you," he said.

"What are you saying?"

"I want us to get married and raise the baby together."

Lydia's heart tumbled to the bottom of her stomach. How had Gunner known that was exactly what she'd been thinking during the drive back to Madison? Except when she'd envisioned him proposing, it hadn't sounded like a business deal.

And therein lay the problem. When Lydia had driven across the Illinois-Wisconsin state line, she'd finally accepted that her love for Gunner wasn't just an infatuation that would go away after she put some distance between them. Hundreds of miles couldn't stop her from loving his laid-back attitude. His goofy obsession with rodeo when he wasn't any good at it. His quick grin and sexy stride. His courage in facing a future he'd never planned for himself.

She was in love with the way he treated his grandfather. With his baby-book reading, lavender oil and fruit-water recipes. So what if he lived in a motel room and didn't have a 401(k)? So what if he didn't have a college degree or if he used a golf club instead of a yard trimmer to knock the heads off dandelions? And because she loved him, she didn't want him to be chained to a life he didn't want.

"I appreciate the offer, Gunner, but you shouldn't have to pay the price for an unplanned pregnancy."

"Sometimes things happen for a reason."

The man was too honorable.

He trailed a finger down her cheek. Then he brushed his mouth against her forehead. "I intend to be a part of my child's life, Lydia."

"I'm not going to keep you away from our baby." She wanted to bury her face in his shirt; instead she settled for playing with one of the pearl snaps, rubbing her fingertip over the glossy stud. "But it's hard to trust that this is the right thing to do when I know marriage and having kids wasn't in your plans."

"It's true that I never pictured myself as a family

man, but life throws curveballs and I'd rather take a swing than let this pitch pass me by."

"My life and my job are in Wisconsin and you and the motel are in Texas." The words rang hollow in her head.

"I get that Stampede isn't the capital of the design world, but—"

"My friends are here as well as my cousins and my parents."

He drew a hand down his face. "We haven't talked about your parents much. Are you close to them?"

Put on the spot, Lydia confessed, "They're busy with the law office, but we spend holidays together."

"I could move up here and look for work."

Now he was being silly. "You can't rodeo in Wisconsin."

"Sure I can. The Mid-States Rodeo Association has events in Ohio and—"

"What about your grandfather?"

"Logan will look after him."

"And the motel?"

"Gramps can hire someone else to manage the place."

The motel was special. It was her and Gunner's project. She didn't like the idea of a stranger running the business.

He's willing to give up everything for you and the baby.

She expelled a frustrated breath. "We can raise our baby together, Gunner, but we don't have to be married to do it."

"I know you believe if you find the perfect man on that dating site, you'll be together forever, but being a perfect match doesn't guarantee a marriage will last. If the reason you love someone is because they have the same interests and goals as you, then it's not real love."

"What do you know about real love?"

His gaze softened as it ran over Lydia. "I know that when I look at you, I feel good inside. And when I kiss you, I forget that your crazy obsession with to-do lists drives me nuts. When I wake up with you in my arms, I think maybe I don't want to go it alone in life." He brushed his thumb over her lip. "And I know that the hollow feeling in my gut when I think about us not being together means I love you."

He walked over to the table and placed his hat on his head. "I'm not running from you or the baby, Lydia. I'll be in Stampede waiting for you when you're ready to come home."

The quiet click of the front door triggered a flood of tears. Gunner had said he loved her, but could she trust that his love was the forever kind and he wasn't just saying it because he wanted them to get married for the baby's sake and get his grandfather off his back?

Lydia reached for her cell phone. When Sadie picked up, she said, "Can you come over after you get off work?"

"I'll have to bring the boys."

"That's fine. And will you see if Scarlett can come, too?"

"What's the matter? You sound like you've been crying."

"I am crying."

"Don't tell me you went through with that stupid idea and joined a dating site and now some guy's hurt your feelings."

"I did, but that's not why I'm crying."

"Then what is it?"

"Gunner Hardell asked me to marry him."

Sadie gasped. "When?"

"Two minutes ago."

"Wow. I can see a lot happened during your trip to Stampede."

"There's more."

"More what?"

"I'm pregnant."

"I'll tell Scarlett to bring the burgers for supper and I'll stop and get some cheese curds." Wisconsin cheese curds made everything better.

After they said their goodbyes, Lydia went into the bedroom, stretched out on the mattress and then blubbered like a baby.

"I STILL CAN'T believe you and Gunner…" Scarlett ran her fingers through her blond locks. Of the three cousins, who were all blondes, Scarlett was the only one who sported a short, sassy hairstyle accentuating her huge brown eyes and high cheekbones, which she'd inherited from her father.

Lydia peeked around the kitchen doorway, making sure her nephews were paying attention to the TV and not listening in on their mother and aunts' conversation. "It just sort of happened."

Sadie popped a cheese curd into her mouth. "The only thing I remember about the Hardell brothers is that Aunt Amelia said they were a wild bunch of hooligans."

"And good-looking," Scarlett said.

Lydia was still in shock after Gunner's visit. He'd driven all the way up to Wisconsin from Texas just to go to a doctor's appointment with her. That showed he cared for her and their baby. He'd confessed that he loved her, but was his love the strong, steady kind or the here-today-and-gone-tomorrow kind?

"You should be happy about being pregnant, not crying." Sadie pointed at Lydia's swollen eyes. "You said you wanted to get married and have children."

"I wanted marriage to come first, then a baby."

"It still can if you accept Gunner's proposal." Scarlett shrugged. "My parents got married because of me."

"Promise you won't tell anyone I told you." Lydia's gaze swung between her cousins. "Aunt Amelia said Uncle Robert got her pregnant and that's why they married."

Sadie glanced at Scarlett. "I thought Aunt Amelia couldn't have children."

"She had several miscarriages and then after a few years they stopped trying."

"That's sad." Sadie pushed the grease-stained bag of curds toward Lydia. "I'm old-fashioned, but I vote you marry Gunner whether you love him or not. For legal reasons it's important that the baby have his last name." She snorted. "Not that it will guarantee child-support payments if you end up divorced."

"I think love is important," Scarlett said. "What if Lydia marries Gunner and then a year later she runs into *the one*?"

Lydia listened to her cousins debate the pros and cons of marrying, but the words didn't register with her brain. "The entire time we were together I compared him to the men on the dating site." She blinked. "And he's nothing like the guys who were matched with me."

"That can be good or bad, you know," Sadie said.

"Look at your mom and dad. They're both lawyers. They finish each other's sentences and they never argue. They're like best friends."

"And that's good?" Lydia asked.

"In some ways, but it's also boring." Scarlett grasped Lydia's hand and squeezed her fingers. "You don't need your husband to be your best friend. You have Sadie and me for that."

"She doesn't need a husband at all," Sadie said. "I'm raising the boys and working and I'm fine."

Scarlett's eyebrow arched. "You are not fine and you know it, but that's a conversation for another time."

"No arguing," Lydia said.

"You're attracted to Gunner or you wouldn't have slept with him. Attraction is important, but I happen to think the best guys are the ones who keep us off balance. Who do the opposite of what we expect," Scarlett said.

That was Gunner in a nutshell. She hadn't counted on him making the trip to Madison. And she sure hadn't expected him to propose to her a second time.

And never in a million years had she expected him to tell her that he loved her.

"Uh-oh," Sadie said when the boys walked into the kitchen. "Looks like it's time to leave before these guys grow bored and tear the place up."

Scarlett looked at her watch. "I should go, too. I've got a spin class at seven and I'm going to need to do a lot of spinning to work off the cheese curds I ate."

Lydia walked everyone to the door, then gave the boys and her cousins a hug. "Thank you for coming over."

"You have much to think about," Sadie said.

"Or not." Scarlett winked.

"I'll keep you posted." Lydia shut the door, then leaned her back against it, Scarlett's words echoing through her brain. If she listened to her head, there wasn't much to think about at all. If she listened to her heart, she had a lot of planning to do.

Chapter Fourteen

"Did Gramps send you over here to check on me?" Gunner set his screwdriver down and climbed to his feet.

"He's too busy chasing after Amelia to worry about you." Logan scowled. "You haven't come out to the ranch since you returned from Wisconsin."

Gunner spread his arms wide. "I've been busy."

"I can see that." He nodded to the crib Gunner had just carried into the motel room. "When did you decide to turn your bachelor pad into a nursery?"

"It's a combination office and nursery." When Lydia visited, Gunner wanted her close by with the baby while he worked, and what better way to keep them near than to give them their own room at the motel?

"The baby furniture looks handmade." Logan examined the dresser and tested the drawers.

"I caught Lydia drooling over this set at the Fourth of July festival in Mesquite. The lady said Lydia had asked about a rocking horse, so they're making one to match the furniture. I have to pick that up next week."

"Isn't this expensive?"

"It wasn't cheap." Gunner had used up most of his savings to buy the furniture.

"And you think converting the room into a nursery will change Lydia's mind about marrying you?"

"Maybe." He hoped it would prove that he'd do anything for her and their baby.

Gunner wished he hadn't returned to Stampede and told his brother and grandfather that he'd proposed to Lydia again and that she'd left him hanging—again. When he'd gotten back to town, he'd sent her a text inviting her to phone anytime she wanted to talk. She'd texted back a Thanks, I'll be in touch, and that was the last he'd heard from her.

He was hoping that when she finally came to terms with her pregnancy, she'd jump at the chance to marry him. But that might not happen right away, so he'd decided to turn his personal room into a quiet retreat for Lydia and the baby when they came to visit. He wanted the space to be comfortable so they'd spend more time in Stampede and give him a chance to court Lydia properly.

"I can't believe after all these years you've given up your room," Logan said.

Gunner had surprised himself, too. The first time Lydia had mentioned renovating room 1, he'd objected. But then he'd figured out why he'd been attached to the room. The number one had been a symbol of his freedom—his desire to remain single. A guy couldn't mess up if he was accountable only to himself. With his family history, Gunner had never wanted to be responsible for anyone else's happiness but his own. There was a lot less pain involved in letting only yourself down versus letting others down.

But Lydia and the baby were changing his mind and he was ready to accept all the responsibility that came with raising a child and being in a committed relationship—the good and the bad. The joy and the pain.

The only way he knew to show Lydia he was ready to leave the old Gunner behind and embrace a new life with her and their baby was to turn his room into their room.

"How did you pay for all this?" Logan asked.

"I didn't charge this on the ranch credit card, if you're worried about that." His brother looked away, but not before Gunner saw the relieved expression on his face. Before he could ask if something was wrong, Logan's phone went off.

While his brother stepped outside to take the call, Gunner went into the bathroom and opened the delivery box containing a baby monitor and video camera that he'd ordered online. He planned to install the camera in the room so if he was watching the baby and needed to go to the office, he could keep an eye on the little tyke.

Logan stepped back into the room and said, "What if all this doesn't impress Lydia?"

"Then I'll keep searching for something that does." He set the camera and monitor on the bed and perused the assembly directions.

"Why didn't you wait until you knew for sure if Lydia would move back to Stampede before spending all this money?"

"She said she wouldn't keep me from being involved in the baby's life. That means I'll have shared custody and I need a safe place for my kid when I work."

"What happens to the baby when you're off rodeoing?"

"I won't rodeo when I have the baby, but if I need to go somewhere, I've got it all figured out," Gunner said.

"How's that?"

"Amelia's offered to babysit if I need her to and she has lady friends in town who are dying to watch the baby, too." He nodded to the phone in his brother's hand. "Who was that?"

"Gramps. He's taking Amelia to Mesquite to try out the new steak house that just opened there."

"Does Gramps want you to chaperone them?"

Logan shook his head. "They're on their own this time."

"I don't get their relationship."

"They've been getting along better since the motel renovations were completed." Logan nodded to the stack of flyers on the bed. "Is Lydia returning for the grand opening?"

"I invited her, but I don't know if she'll come." If she didn't show up, then Gunner would make another trip to Wisconsin and another and another until he convinced her to come back with him.

Logan nodded to the crib. "For what it's worth, I think you'll be a great dad."

The door closed, leaving Gunner alone in the room with his doubts.

"PIPE DOWN NOW so I can get this speech over with."

Lydia swallowed a laugh as Emmett stood in the bed of his old jalopy in front of the Moonlight Motel and squinted into the afternoon sunlight.

After arriving in town a few minutes ago, Lydia had driven to the motel and parked the rental car behind the long line of vehicles on the shoulder of the highway.

She'd slipped into the crowd, wearing a floppy hat and sunglasses, hoping no one would recognize her and coerce her into giving a speech.

Emmett cleared his throat and the crowd quieted. "The Moonlight Motel has been a part of Stampede for decades and I thought it looked just fine the way it was, but Ms. Amelia Rinehart said it needed a facelift." Applause echoed through the group.

"I bought this place for my wife, Sara. She said it brought back memories of her family vacations as a child." Emmett wiped the sweat from his brow. "Sara always wanted to see this place fixed up and I know she'd be real proud of the way it looks now." He cleared his throat again. "Since Amelia Rinehart is responsible for this renovation, she might as well be the one to talk about it." Emmett extended his hand to Lydia's aunt, who climbed the makeshift steps up to the truck bed. While her aunt chatted about the Hollywood-movie themes for the rooms, Lydia's eyes searched for Gunner.

It took only a moment to find his broad shoulders in the crowd. He wore a sky blue Western shirt, his cowboy hat and her favorite jeans of his—the pair with a rip in the back pocket. Beads of perspiration dotted her upper lip—she was nervous, excited and scared all at once. Her heart had known the moment Gunner had left the apartment a few weeks ago that she'd be back in Stampede. It had just taken a little longer to convince her brain that he was her perfect match. Once she'd let go of the fear, she'd known in her heart that she and Gunner and their baby were meant to be together.

"I wish I could take all the credit for this wonderful remodel, but my great-niece Lydia Canter designed the rooms, and many thanks to Karl Schmidt and Emmett's grandson Gunner. They did most of the heavy lifting." More applause.

"I hope you'll stay and look at the rooms, then help yourself to the barbecue on the patio behind the motel. Please tell your friends and family to book a room at the Moonlight the next time they visit Stampede. And just so you know—" Amelia glanced at Emmett, who looked bored to death "—this is only the beginning of our plans to revitalize our town." Amelia turned off the microphone and Lydia couldn't hear whatever Emmett grumbled in her aunt's ear.

The older couple climbed down from the truck bed, then went into the office—probably to argue over the next renovation project her aunt had up her sleeve. The crowd dispersed to check out the rooms, but Lydia's attention focused on Gunner, who remained behind in the parking lot. He must have sensed her presence, because he turned around.

His eyes widened as she walked toward him. "You came for the reveal," he said.

She pulled in a steadying breath. "I came for you. For us. For our baby." If she hadn't been so nervous, she might have laughed at his incredulous expression.

"Are you saying what I think you're saying?"

She smiled, cursing her shaky lips. "Yes. I'll marry you, Gunner. And yes, I'll move to Stampede."

He pulled her into his arms and she buried her face against his shirt. "I'll do my best to make you not regret this."

She slipped her arms around his waist. "The only thing I regret is not listening to my heart sooner."

"What do you mean?"

She looked him in the eye. "I love you, Gunner.

I loved you before I found out I was pregnant. I just wouldn't give you a chance because—"

"I don't fit with any of the dating profiles you were looking at?"

His eyes shone with laughter.

"Actually, I discovered I'd been using the wrong criteria when searching for possible husband candidates." She smiled. "I need a man who will make me laugh and won't let me work too hard. I need a man who will show me how to enjoy the little things in life."

"Then I'm your man." He reached under the brim of her hat and tucked a strand of loose hair behind her ear. "And I need you to hold my feet to the fire and make me accountable."

"Then I'm your woman."

"We can live in Wisconsin if you want. As long as we're together, I don't care where we settle down," he said.

There was so much more to Gunner than he let others see and Lydia was just discovering the extent of his generosity.

"Stampede has grown on me. And Aunt Amelia isn't going to be around forever—neither is your grandfather. I think we should live here and raise our child."

He hugged her tight.

"You can keep rodeoing and I'll work on my interior-design business while I watch over the motel."

"You're not making all the sacrifices, Lydia. I may pick up a rodeo here or there, but I'm done trying to make a living at it. I'm ready to manage the motel and start pulling my weight."

"But I want you to be happy," she said.

"I enjoy rodeo, but I love you. When you became

pregnant, I realized that my life had been going no-where for a long time. You and the baby have given me purpose and direction. I'll manage the motel and you manage your decorating business."

She stood on tiptoe and kissed him.

"I have something to show you." He took her hand and led her to room 1, then slid a keycard through the new card-reader lock and opened the door.

Lydia stepped inside and gasped. "Oh, Gunner." Tears stung her eyes. "It's beautiful." She walked over to the crib and trailed her fingers across the rail. "How did you know?"

"I saw you looking at the furniture at the rodeo. I got the lady's card before I caught up with you. After you left, I contacted her and we struck a deal." He brushed a tear from her cheek. "I figured no matter what happened between us that you'd honor your word and allow me to be a part of the baby's life. I wanted to have a place close by for both of you when you visited."

Gunner nodded to the vintage desk he'd found at a flea market. "I thought you could do your design work here while the baby's sleeping."

"What happened to your grandmother's rocking chair?"

"It's still in the office." He shrugged. "If I'm tak-ing care of the baby and watching the front desk at the same time, I figured it would come in handy if I had to feed the little bugger."

An image of Gunner rocking their baby brought more tears to her eyes. "Is that a camera?" She pointed to the ceiling.

"Yep. You can see everything in the room on the monitor at the front desk. There's another camera in the office, so I'll know if anyone walks in while I'm here with the baby—" he waggled an eyebrow "—or you."

Life with Gunner would never be dull. Lydia poked her head into the bathroom and saw the baby tub and water toys. "You thought of everything." She hugged him. "I can't believe you turned your bachelor pad into a nursery."

"I can't believe you turned this cowboy into a daddy." He kissed her, then tilted his head toward the brand-new double bed.

"It needs to be christened," he said.

She struggled not to smile. "How can I refuse such a romantic invitation?"

Gunner walked over to the door and threw the bolt, then closed the curtains.

They tumbled onto the mattress. Clothes landed haphazardly on the floor as their kisses grew heated, their touches more urgent. Then they froze when someone knocked.

"Gunner, you in there?"

"I'm busy, Gramps."

"Doing what?"

"He's busy with me, Mr. Hardell."

"Lydia? Is that you?" her aunt called.

Gunner grinned.

"It's me, Aunt Amelia."

"Are you and Gunner…?"

"Yes, Aunt Amelia."

"C'mon, Emmett, leave the lovebirds alone."

"It's the middle of the day. That ain't decent."

"Stop being such a fuddy-duddy. You were young once. You remember what it felt like to…"

Lydia giggled and buried her face in Gunner's neck.

"Everyone out there will know what we're doing," Gunner said.

"Forget about them and kiss me."

Gunner obliged and an hour later Lydia fell asleep, her last thought being that she had to check her bank statement to make sure SavvyMatch.com had canceled her membership fee.

* * * * *

*If you loved this novel, don't miss
the next book by Marin Thomas in the*
COWBOYS OF STAMPEDE, TEXAS *series!
Available September 2017
from Harlequin Western Romance!*

#1645 WANTED: TEXAS DADDY
Texas Legacies: The Lockharts
by Cathy Gillen Thacker

Sage Lockhart and Nick Monroe are friends with benefits.
When Sage asks Nick to make her dream of having a family
come true, he agrees...only because he is secretly in love
with her!

#1646 THE RANCHER'S SURPRISE BABY
Blue Falls, Texas • by Trish Milburn

Rancher Ben Hartley has never wanted kids after a horrible
childhood, but then he gets Mandy Richardson pregnant.
What if the thing he fears most turns out to be the best thing
that's ever happened to him?

#1647 A BABY ON HIS DOORSTEP
by Roz Denny Fox

Rodeo cowboy Rio McNabb is recovering from injuries, and
his nurse, Binney Taylor, is driving him crazy. But his life gets
even more intense when a strange woman drops off a baby,
claiming he's the father.

#1648 A COWBOY TO KISS
by Mary Leo

Kenzie Grant is trying her best to save the family ranch.
When Jake Scott disagrees with her methods, sparks fly—
not only about the ranch but with each other!

HWESTCNM0517

Get 2 Free Books,

Plus 2 Free Gifts—
just for trying the Reader Service!

*Sage Lockhart and Nick Monroe are friends with
benefits. When Sage asks Nick to make her dream of
having a family come true, he agrees...only because he
is secretly in love with her!*

*Read on for a sneak preview of
WANTED: TEXAS DADDY,
the latest book in Cathy Gillen Thacker's series
TEXAS LEGACIES: THE LOCKHARTS.*

"You want to have my baby," Nick Monroe repeated
slowly, leading the two saddled horses out of the stables.

Sage Lockhart slid a booted foot into the stirrup and
swung herself up. She'd figured the Monroe Ranch was
the perfect place to have this discussion. Not only was it
Nick's ancestral home, but with Nick the only one living
there now, it was completely private.

She drew her flat-brimmed hat straight across her
brow. "An unexpected request, I know."

Yet, she realized as she studied him, noting that the
color of his eyes was the same deep blue as the big Texas
sky above, he didn't look all that shocked.

For he better than anyone knew how much she wanted a
child. They'd grown quite close ever since she'd returned
to Texas, to claim her inheritance from her late father and
help her mother weather a scandal that had rocked the
Lockhart family to the core.

HWREXP0517

She drew a deep, bolstering breath. "The idea of a complete stranger fathering my child is becoming increasingly unappealing." When they reached their favorite picnic spot, she swung herself out of the saddle and watched as Nick tied their horses to a tree.

Nick grinned, as if pleased to hear she was a one-man woman, at least in this respect.

He looked at her from beneath the brim of his hat. "Which is why you're asking me?" he countered in the rough, sexy tone she'd fallen in love with the first second she had heard it. "Because you know me?"

Sage locked eyes with him, not sure whether he was teasing her or not. One thing she knew for sure: there hadn't been a time since they'd first met that she *hadn't* wanted him.

"Or because," he continued flirtatiously, as he unscrewed the lid on his thermos, "you have a hankering for my DNA?"

Aware the only appetite she had now was not for food, she quipped, "How about both?"

Don't miss WANTED: TEXAS DADDY
by Cathy Gillen Thacker, available June 2017 wherever
Harlequin® Western Romance
books and ebooks are sold.

www.Harlequin.com